GW00457006

Hello you!

Thank you so much to all the people who have supported me whilst I create this novel, I am so incredibly grateful.

I would also be forever thankful if you wouldn't mind leaving me a little review on Amazon when you have finished.

I hope you enjoy it!

Lots of love,

Chloe

Chapter one

Divorced. It's official. I'm thirty-six years old and divorced.

I study the papers in my hands over and over again and allow myself a moment to feel sadness over the words. A tear effortlessly falls down my cheek as I recall our six years of marriage. Not because I miss him, or even because it's over, but because I feel as though I wasted so much time. That's the worst feeling – realising that over eight years of my life were spent with the wrong person. It just makes that part of my life feel so void.

I met Alex at a New Year's Eve party years ago. I was fresh out of university and a newly qualified sports journalist. I landed on my feet pretty quickly and managed to get myself a job working as a sports columnist for a popular newspaper. It was at my new job, I started networking and meeting new people, particularly famous athletes. I was star-struck each time. This lifestyle was fast paced and more glamorous than I had ever anticipated. A lot of the athletes threw over-the-top house parties, particularly the younger footballers and rugby players. They were notorious for it. Around Christmas time, Alex messaged me out of the blue on my social media account. He told me how he had been reading my columns and really enjoyed my style of writing and my passion for sports. Alex was a well-known Welsh rugby player – one of the best not only for his club, but his country.

It made me nervous to see his name appear in my messages, it was surreal. I had been dreaming of this world since I was in my early teenage years. I dreamt of meeting these kinds of people and immersing myself in the world of sports and getting the opportunity to meet such talented and brilliant athletes, but I never once dreamt it could be like this.

I giggle a little as I think back to his first-ever message to me.

Wow. I have been reading your columns now for quite some time and before I clocked the feminine name, I always pictured some old bloke with a grey beard and pipe who spends his weekends going to local cricket matches and betting on the horses. And yet here you are. Quite the opposite. Can I take you out on a date? Unless of course you do have a beard and a pipe?

The last line of that message made me smile from ear to ear. It was from this point that our relationship started. I agreed to go on a date with Alex and I accompanied him to a New Year's Eve party hosted by an ex-England footballer; it was one of the best nights of my life. I met so many sports heroes of mine and drank the best champagne and partied with some big names. It was magical.

As was Alex. I was in awe of him. He was popular, funny and kind. We went onto have a really fun relationship. We were in love, but we were also young. Young with a lot of money. We went on holidays – skiing in the Alps, shopping in New York, sunbathing in Hawaii and flying first class to other countries I never dreamt I would visit. Then, on my thirtieth birthday, everything changed when Alex got down on one knee in the middle of a packed Miami Beach and proposed to me. How could I say no? We seemingly had it all. We were in love, we were having so much fun, I had my career, he had his, and together we were thriving.

Until, that is, Alex had suffered a serious injury a few months after our wedding.

He wasn't playing rugby when it happened but riding his first motorbike. He bought a Harley-Davidson on a whim one day and thought he'd take it for a spin as soon as it was delivered. It was his dream to one day ride Route 66 on a Harley. He had no previous experience, no clue really on how to ride a bike but he was convinced it was easy enough and so off he went.

Nearly forty minutes later, I had the police at my door to tell me there had been a serious accident and Alex had crashed into the back of a truck in one of the country lanes.

He was airlifted to a top London hospital and although they managed to stabilise him quickly, his injuries were so serious that he would need years of support and physio to correct all the damage he had done. I knew straightaway that his rugby career was over. I worried deeply about how he would react to a life without playing rugby and fulfilling the goals he had been working towards for so long, but nothing could prepare me for the reality of what was to become of him.

As the months turned into years, the Alex I had known and loved became virtually non-existent. The new Alex relied heavily on whiskey just to get out of bed in the morning and spent most of his days treating me as though he hated me.

Every day, I felt guilty. I still had my career, my columns were becoming more popular, my social life was thriving, and I was still part of the glamorous life of professional athletics with all the parties and fun that go along with it. But Alex refused to attend anything sports related once his career came to an end. Sports became a forbidden topic in our house. I loved Alex but nothing I did made him any happier. Nothing gave him back any of the drive and the ambition that he used to have.

The arguments got worse – he hated me for being a part of that life without him and for continuing to be a sports journalist. His drinking became heavier and it got to the point where I couldn't remember a time when I had seen him sober.

I pleaded with him to put down the bottle and to fight for us, for our relationship. But Alex wasn't interested.

The only thing he would do was lock himself away in one of the rooms he turned into a man cave and drink himself into an abyss. I use the term man cave loosely, it was really just a room with a sofa, built-in bar and mini fridge.

The last straw came one bank holiday weekend when he got so drunk that his anger grew uncontrollable. He started blaming me for everything that had gone so wrong in his life and, in front of my eyes, he began smashing up our home. He said he didn't deserve any of the nice things we had worked hard for and neither did I. He threw our photo frames against walls, he put a golf club through our television and our cabinets, he smashed every cup and plate in the kitchen and bellowed that I was to blame whilst he did it. Then he turned to me, his eyes filled with venom and his body language fuelled by hate and raised his hand to me. He stopped himself at the last second and punched the wall next to me instead. But it was enough.

Our marriage was over; I wasn't going to spend my life as the villain in Alex's story anymore. I had to get out.

I secretly hoped for a little while that the start of the divorce proceedings would prompt Alex into fighting for me, for us. But nothing happened. I packed up and left Alex in our six-bed home in London and headed for a temporary apartment near Crystal Palace. It wasn't luxury but it was better than a life walking on eggshells with Alex.

My dad used to say that football is a game made up of two forty-five-minute halves. Sometimes the first half of the match indicates everything you can expect from the game, but occasionally, and most excitingly, a second half can be truly unpredictable.

Take the 2011 Newcastle vs Arsenal game for example. In the first half, Arsenal managed to score four goals and looked very much as though they were going to win the game with ease –

most would have expected Arsenal to finish with eight goals to nil, or something equally theatrical. And as the second half got underway, most of the Newcastle fans started leaving the stadium as their chances looked ever bleaker as time went on. But unbelievably, Newcastle managed to score four goals, with the last goal being scored in the very last minute of the game. The stadium was electric. It was a brilliant and entertaining comeback, one which would go down in history. Which is just like life really.

I wipe the tear from my eye and carefully tuck away the divorce papers in a plastic folder. As I close the folder, I can't help but smile a little as I hear my dad's voice in my head: brush yourself off sweetheart, we have the second half to play.

Chapter two

"Yes, Mum." I sigh, but really, I find her fussing over me to be quite comforting.

"Just don't forget to text me as soon as you are settled and unpacked, I can't wait for a little video tour," Mum excitedly squeals into the handset. "And? What else are you going to be doing?"

"I know, I know," I reply as I roll my eyes. "I'll be getting the locks changed straightaway."

"Yes, please make sure you do. I know you're the owner now, but you never know who had a set of keys before and maybe even who had keys before that person. You don't want some creep letting themselves in, do you?" Mum asks seriously and I can't help but giggle.

I'm used to Mum fussing down the phone by now. It's the only relationship with her I have known. My mum works on the cruise ships as a singer – she's currently giving me my orders from the Bahamas. When her and my dad got married, she promised she would give up working on the cruise liners and get a job near home instead, but I guess it was a promise she couldn't keep. When she fell pregnant with me, she again promised my dad she would give up travelling the world and singing to help raise me, but somehow, she managed to get Dad to agree that she should continue working away. My dad pretty much raised me single-handedly and I adored him for it. He was a patient man – well, he'd have to be to put up with my mum's stubbornness and always having to accept that her career came before either of us.

Despite all of that, my dad adored her. He would never stand in the way of her dreams. He stood by her and supported her every step of the way, even if it meant that for six to seven months out of the year he was without his wife and I was without my mum.

I still struggle to think about him without getting emotional. My dad suffered a major stroke a few months before I met Alex. I coped okay, all things considered, but occasionally I still struggle with loneliness. Even knowing that Dad had passed away and I was now on my own didn't prompt Mum to stay at home for very long. Within a few months she was off again, heading for the Caribbean and not looking back. She kept saying that it's what my dad would have wanted. I had no choice but to learn how to be independent and take care of myself. Apart from when I was with Alex, it's only ever been me. I've had to learn to be my own best friend.

I do love my mum's phone calls whenever she does have the time to ring me, although it's usually just her telling me how well a performance went or how amazing the weather is in whichever country they've docked at. Then, after a quick chat, she hangs up and that's it for another month or two. I think that's why I can't help but giggle on the phone to her – she tries hard to mother me sometimes, but those days are long gone. I see her as a friend really and if she was honest, I think she would probably say that's how she views me too. Motherhood had never suited her, nor had it been on her life's agenda, and that's fine. She did the best she could.

"I'll be fine Mum," I say with a smile. "Don't worry about a thing. I'll try and call you when I'm all settled."

"Okay Mia. If I don't answer it's because I'm at sea and you know what the internet can be like. I'll just get back to you as soon as I can."

"I know, I'll look forward to it." I smile again. I've heard her say that a million times before.

When I've hung up my phone, I grab the last packing box and another suitcase and drag it behind me as I make my way to my car. I place them in the boot of my Lexus and eagerly get into the front seat and set up my satnav. Even though I have driven myself to the new house a couple of times already for the viewings, I'm a little bit hazy with the directions and don't want to get lost. It's not the easiest place to find.

My new house in Hertfordshire is nearly a two-hour drive from London, right out of the way in a quiet suburb. It's beautiful and just what I need. I never really imagined I would live in a suburb, I always pictured myself staying in the centre of London, but after all the drama with Alex, I'm ready for a different pace of life. I want to spend my evenings sipping red wine and writing my columns from my pretty garden, overlooking fields and watching the sunset. I want to get away from the hustle of the city and concentrate on myself for a while. It's the best decision I could have made for myself.

The drive is relaxing – the sun is shining and there isn't a cloud in the sky. I love this time of year; spring is beautiful in England. I catch my reflection in my wing mirror and for the first time in a year I like what I see. My short blonde hair is down and wavy; I put a little hairspray in it this morning but mostly I let it sit naturally, a bit of a fresh-from-the beach kind of look. This is why I love this time of year: I find it easier to look and feel good. My skin is a little sun kissed and I love the slight tanned glow against my white Bardot top which hangs slightly off my shoulders. I throw on my sunglasses and my heart skips a beat. I am excited. I feel like the fire inside of me is back. I like who I am again and most importantly I'm loving my life again.

I keep the car windows down all the way and enjoy the fresh country air lightly blowing against my face. The closer I get to the house, the more green everything becomes. So many farms and fields surround me, everything is so open and picturesque.

I can now switch off my satnav as I'm on the single-lane country road that leads towards my house. I guess you would describe where I live as a cul-de-sac although it's very small. It only has five houses on it, and I was told by the estate agent that two of them are used as holiday homes only, so it is usually very quiet.

"Wow," I say to myself as I stare at my new house. The way the sun is hitting the glass makes it look even better than last time. My house is the smallest on this little cul-de-sac but the most modern. Instead of walls, it is all panelled glass which is what pulled me towards it in the first place. I love the thought of my house being filled with natural light, so this was a no-brainer for me. Both the downstairs and upstairs have glass all across it instead of brick.

I pull my car into the driveway and just sit studying its every feature. It really is breath-taking. You can see right into my house but obviously that's what blinds are for, on the off chance that I need my privacy, although apart from the house opposite, nobody should really be able to see in as I have a couple of tall trees and bushes around the sides to help maintain some seclusion.

The house opposite is the biggest here, it's easily a seven- or eight-bedroom house and it's beautiful. It's fairly modern but still has an older rustic charm about it. It doesn't have the glass style like mine, it's a lot more private and set back but has a very grand feel.

I quickly pull the door keys out of my bag and let myself in. The double front doors open up and the warmth hits me straightaway. The sun has spilled through the windows so much it's heated up the entire house like a little sun trap. I kick off my shoes and let my bare feet feel the cool tiled floor beneath me. I rush around the house and excitedly push open the veranda doors and let the fresh air in. It really is exquisite.

I feel like a child in a sweet shop. I truly don't know what I want to do first. The more mature side of me thinks I should unpack and get organised, but the other more laid-back side wants to celebrate with a few glasses of red wine and to light some scented candles and just bask in this moment. Laid-back Mia wins. Without giving it another moment's thought, I'm already reaching into my bag for my bottle of wine.

After I pour myself a large glass, I send my mum a quick text message to let her know I made it safe and sound. Typically, the text doesn't deliver – she rarely gets a signal whilst on the cruise ships.

I take a big slurp of my wine and head out onto the patio in the garden. The late afternoon sun beams down onto my skin which immediately calms me and makes me feel happy. This is pure bliss.

I can't hear any of the usual traffic sounds or police sirens, nothing but the birds singing and the breeze gently rustling through the trees around me.

Tomorrow I'll probably make a start with setting up my office. My new desk and other furniture arrive tomorrow so I can spend the day organising myself. Now that I'll be working from home part-time, I'll need to crack on and get myself set up.

A little rustle in the bush breaks me from my thoughts and a beautiful petite light grey cat comes bouncing over to me.

"Aww... Hello puss." I smile as the friendly little cat rubs her face against my legs and purrs heavily.

"You are simply adorable, aren't you?" I continue in what can only be described as a weird high-pitched baby voice. I have been in my new house for approximately an hour now and I have already made a new friend. So far so good. She lies down next to me and continues purring whilst enjoying all the attention I am giving her.

I'm not sure where she has come from but I'm quite pleased that she's found her way into my garden.

"So, puss, what's your name? My name is Mia," I say in my ridiculous baby voice, which makes me giggle to myself as I imagine how crazy I would look if someone could see me now. A crazy cat lady no doubt.

"Well puss...since you asked, I'm thirty-six years old and newly divorced. Yep. I know. I'm young and I'm divorced. But you know what puss? I'm going to be okay. Really, I am. And you know what else? Alex didn't deserve me. Sometimes you have to remember your worth. Worth is important. You know?" I babble on enthusiastically, sipping at my wine in between breaths.

"I mean...am I worried about being lonely out here, you ask? Not at all. Well maybe a little. But hey, I have you now, don't I, puss? That's all I need. Just me, newly divorced, single Mia and her new friend, a cat called...Puss." I smirk at myself as I glance behind me and realise that the bottle of red on the kitchen counter is almost empty and I haven't eaten all day. I can always tell when I'm getting tipsy because I talk really fast and, for some unknown reason, I seem to refer to myself in the third person a lot.

Good one Mia. First night in your new home and you get shit-faced and tell a stray cat your life story. Excellent work. I pull myself onto my feet and head back inside. My legs are a little wobbly, but I do my best to walk as if I am completely sober.

"Night Puss. I better get to bed," I say before closing the patio doors behind me. "See you again soon."

Chapter three

I wake up quite refreshed considering I drank a bottle of wine on an empty stomach. My furniture arrived bright and early so most of my day will be spent organising myself as planned. I start with the lounge area which takes the longest. I hang lots of pictures and my mirror to make it feel as though my stamp is on the house, and I arrange my sofa, coffee table, lamps and television just how I want them.

I stop for a quick bite for lunch and then spend the afternoon in my office, setting up my desk and arranging all my files and preparing myself for work. It needed to be done because next week I'll be starting to work from home a lot more and I know if I don't do it now, I never will. I'll get around to finishing my bedroom and bathroom as soon as I can. They're not as important.

The kitchen doesn't need anything doing to it thankfully, it's been newly fitted with all the little features and elegant touches I need and is already equipped with a double oven and a huge American fridge freezer. I already spent ten minutes this morning fascinated by the ice dispenser on the front.

All the walls are lightly coloured with a cream paint, and a couple of accent walls are papered with gold lining. It fits perfectly with my taste, which is another reason I chose this house whilst on my search. It felt ready to move into and needed very little work doing to it. I'm not exactly clued up with DIY, so it suits me well.

My huge windows also got fitted with long transparent white drapes today. I might look into fitting some electronic blackout blinds eventually, but for now I'm happy enough with the sheer drapes. It is very private here after all. Waking up to the sun shining down on my bed this morning was as wonderful as I had hoped. I spent ten minutes just sitting up in my bed and gazing out through my glass wall. This is my forever home. I can feel it. I can't think of a single reason why I would ever want to leave here.

As I give the house a well-needed hoover, I feel myself growing tired. It's been quite a long day and I think all the excitement of moving has finally caught up with me. I haven't picked a home for the hoover yet so I tuck it to one side in the hallway and decide it can wait as right now I deserve a nice long soak in the tub. I gather my best bath salts and head for the bathroom. I have been waiting for this moment ever since I first saw the house. The bath is an egg-shaped stone bath and looks so incredibly inviting. I grab half a dozen white fluffy towels from a moving box and stack them up neatly on the bathroom shelves. I grab a bottle of bubble bath too and throw in a generous amount as the bath begins to fill.

I quickly strip off and carefully climb into the bath. The warm water feels so good against my skin. My lower back has been aching all afternoon and my shoulders have been so tense, but as I ease myself into this bath, I feel my muscles relaxing and it's a welcome relief. I'm not the type of person who has a quick bath, I never have been. Alex used to call me his little mermaid because I could be in the bath for pretty much an hour most nights. God, my face screws up as I realise my thoughts have wondered into Alex territory again. I suppose it's normal, considering the length of time we were together, but I'm looking forward to the days when my mind doesn't automatically jump to memories of my ex-husband.

Bollocks. All the lights in the house have gone off. I didn't even realise the sun had gone down until I found myself sitting here in darkness. It must be a power cut. Damn it. I usually light candles when I have a bath – the one night I couldn't be bothered to do it, there's a power cut.

I quickly get out of the bath and carefully make my way to the shelves and grab a white towel. I flick the bathroom light switch on and off but nothing. I go into the hallway and the bedroom and try to turn the lights on in there too, but I'm still in the dark. It must definitely be a power cut. I'm sure I had a torch in one of the boxes somewhere and a bag of tea lights. If I can just find those then I'll at least have some light for a little while.

Suddenly I hear a knock at the door. Bollocks. Who could that be?

"I'm, erm, I'm coming, two minutes," I call as I quickly rush into my bedroom to find some clothes.

It's too dark though and I can barely see a thing. I wouldn't even know what I was putting on. Knowing my luck, I'd pull out an old bridesmaid dress from the nineties or something and go downstairs looking like Bo Peep. Another knock at the door. Shit.

"I'm coming..." I call again.

Sod it, I'll have to go down in my towel. How embarrassing.

Fuck fuck fuck, I mutter to myself as I hurry out of my bedroom.

"OW! Shiiiiiiit," I gasp as I stub my toe on the hoover which I had forgotten I left in the hallway.

"Bloody dickhead *hoover*. Ouch ouch ouch! Fuck fuck fuck," I whine to myself as I limp down the stairs.

I swing my front door open whilst keeping one hand firmly on my towel to make sure I don't flash whoever is at my door.

"Hi!" A beautiful red-headed woman greets me with a huge Julia

Roberts-style smile. "I'm Elle and this is my husband Jacob. We're your new neighbours."

Jesus, she's immaculate. Her hair is neatly styled, and she's dressed in a skirt suit. She looks so posh.

"Hi…" I say, a little flustered after having rushed down the stairs. "I'm Mia. I moved in yesterday."

"Yeah, my husband saw you arriving and so I thought we should come and introduce ourselves, and then of course there was a power cut which tends to happen around here, so we thought we had better come now and make sure you're okay," she informs me pleasantly. She's very well-spoken. Somehow, I already know she's from the huge house opposite.

"I'm Jacob. It's nice to see someone our age has finally moved to the area," he subtly jokes with a smile. He sounds friendly but his demeanour very much suggests he was forced by his wife to come over and say hello.

Jacob is undeniably handsome. He looks like he just walked right out of an Abercrombie and Fitch catalogue. He dresses very smartly too, wearing a white fitted shirt. Very fitted actually. His shoulders are broad, his arms, big…manly. His dark hair is wavy but styled back, his eyes are big and brown. Jesus Christ, I think I'm staring.

Stop staring Mia, I think to myself.

"Ah, yes! That was me." I smile back.

"Well welcome to the area! We won't keep you – we didn't realise you were in the bath." Elle giggles as she glances at my towel. "Perhaps we'll come by another time. But you're okay, yeah?"

"Yes, that would be lovely." I smile back, grateful for her kindness. "Oh, and I'm fine, obviously a power cut during a bath isn't the best timing, but I have candles somewhere…"

"Oh good. It's just we heard you saying fuck fuck fuck...and then calling your husband a dickhead," Elle interrupts with another giggle.

"Ah. Yes that." I try to laugh along and mask my embarrassment. "Actually, I'm not married. I'm just...me. Just Mia."

"Oh? So, who were you calling a dickhead?" Elle asks curiously.

"Um..." I shift awkwardly in my towel. "The hoover. It was dark...and I stubbed my toe on it. So, I called it a dickhead."

"Do you often call your hoover a dickhead?" Jacob asks as he stares at me intently.

"Only if it starts it first," I sarcastically blurt which makes Jacob laugh. His demeanour instantly changes, almost as if he is now pleased that he has had to come and introduce himself.

As soon as he laughs, I feel butterflies in my stomach like some teenage girl with a school crush. When he smiles like that, I notice a little dimple on his left cheek. He kind of reminds me of Christian from that movie...*Fifty Shades of Grey*. Elle is a lucky woman. She is very beautiful herself though, and together they look like one hell of a couple. I must look like a hippy stood next to them right now, my blonde hair all dishevelled and my skin dripping wet. I might have to make a point of bumping into them very soon when I look a little more put together. First impressions and all that.

"Actually, we were going to do a little barbecue tomorrow, if you fancy joining us?" Elle offers.

"Oh!" I nod enthusiastically although taken by surprise. "That would be great. I'd love to."

"Perfect. We live just over there," Elle informs me as she gestures to the big house opposite mine. Just as I suspected.

"Okay, great. Would you like me to bring anything?"

"No, no. You're fine. You're our guest. See you at lunchtime then," Elle responds as her smile lights up her face.

Jacob offers a small smile before turning away and heading back to the house. Elle happily waves goodbye as she follows on behind. Just as I close the door, all of the lights suddenly come back on in the house.

I hurry back upstairs and head back into the bathroom. Well, the suburbs are definitely home to some friendly people. Back in London, I don't think my neighbours ever even acknowledged me. I wonder what Elle does for a living; she looks so glamorous but authoritative. Maybe I'll find out tomorrow.

Chapter four – Jacob's Point of view

I fill up the car with nearly a hundred pounds worth of diesel, usually I only stick in fifty, but I'll take whatever keeps me out of the house a few minutes longer.

The living arrangements at home are becoming unbearable. It's like Elle doesn't even try anymore.

At least in the past she got involved with random projects from jewellery parties with her friends and even the odd charity fundraiser. Well, as long as she didn't have to actually get her hands dirty anyway. She looked to look as though she was some Mother Theresa, as long as she didn't have to physically partake. Elle is a lot like my mother-in-law in that sense. I think Elle must have been programmed from a young age to think more about appearances and what she looks like to the world more than anything else.

I always knew this about Elle, right from the very start, so god knows why it grates on me so much now, but it does. There just has to be more to life than this shallow representation of happiness. Which is mostly just a lie anyway. Sure, we have money, we have a great house and we're fortunate. But has it made me happy? Personally, no.

Whilst I wait patiently in the queue inside the petrol station, I surprise myself as a thought of our new neighbour pops into my mind, Mia.

She was surprising. I think she's the first person I have met that openly admits to arguing with a household appliance and smiling as she says it.

When I catch my reflection in the glass of the drink's refrigerator, I realise I'm smiling. Awkwardly, I try to shrug it off. I can't remember the last time something or someone made me smile to myself whilst I'm out on my own.

Another surprise to come from my brief encounter with Mia.

Now I can't help but think about her more. The way she opened the door with her skin slightly wet and glistening. The way her hair was messy but in a way that looked almost on purpose; and sexy.

The way she carelessly stood talking to us in her towel, Elle would have hated that and not just because it was only a towel, but because she would have wanted to be dressed head to toe in her finest clothing, matching shoes and bag, the works. Elle is never careless.

As much as these thoughts had me smiling, they soon begin to irritate me. If I have learned anything from being married to Elle, it's that I don't find relationships easy. I have learned that I am just not one of those people who fall in love like some Nicholas Sparks movie and live happily ever after. I struggle to tolerate most people at the best of times and if I wasn't pressured into getting married so young by my family, then I would for sure be single now; and probably happier for it.

I can't allow intrusive thoughts of the new neighbour to have me questioning my marriage more than I already do. I don't care for the extra complication.

I'm getting by with my life just fine by going to work and coming home. It's boring, drama free but I'm in control of that. What Elle does whilst I am working is something, I stopped concerning myself with a long time ago.
I tried asking her not to spend so much money on our credit cards, but she never listens, and I gave up trying in the end. So now, we are just two people, co-existing and it works for us.

Elle is happy, she has the financial security and the status she desperately craved. Her parents are happy because of that.
I'm content, because I can concentrate on my work and for the most part Elle leaves me alone to get on with it. My parents are happy because they think I married well.
So, there you go, it's not perfect, but everyone is, happy.

Chapter five

Quarter past ten in the morning the clock on my bedside table reads as I stretch out my arms and legs. I sit up and rub my eyes. I hadn't meant to sleep for this long, but I must have needed it.

"Shit," I gasp to myself. I'm supposed to be at the neighbours' house for twelve o'clock, Elle invited me over for their little barbecue. I quickly pull the covers off and head downstairs for a glass of water and ice – I need it to wake me up a little and then I can focus on getting ready. I really want to make an effort today, I'm not sure why. A part of me thinks it's because I want to impress Elle, she looked so put together and elegant when she came to my door last night. In many ways she reminded of a red-haired version of Kate Middleton. She could most certainly pass for someone in the Royal family.

"Morning Puss," I say with a smile as I see the sweet little grey cat standing at my patio door.

I open the patio doors and she comes strolling in without hesitation which makes me laugh.

"Looks like I've made my first friend here in the suburbs," I say affectionately before putting down a little milk for her. "But on that note, I better get ready."

It's another beautiful day. The skies are blue, not a cloud in sight, and although it's still only morning it already feels pretty hot and humid. I head straight for my wardrobe and browse through the selection of dresses I have managed to put away already.

Perfect. I spot a red floral plunge dress. It's girly and pretty and I have always gotten compliments when I have worn it in the past. I pair it with some nude sandal wedges and hoop earrings. I love the way the dress feels once I slip it over my head and pull it down my body. It clings in all the right places. It finishes just above the knee, a little sexy but still quite conservative. I really like it.

I think I'll go for natural make-up today; I dive into my make-up bag and pull out a tinted moisturiser and apply it all over. It gives me a healthy glow without too much coverage. I grab my new mascara and give my lashes a little length and then finish with subtle blush and soft nude lipstick. I lightly scrunch some hair product through my blonde waves and give them a little beach look again.

I'm proud as I study my reflection. This is the first time since Alex that I have made a real effort with my appearance and I feel amazing. My confidence has slowly been creeping back over the past couple of weeks, but right now I feel the best I have felt in a long time. It makes me really smile.

I finish a few more last-minute touches and find myself heading to the big house opposite. Suddenly, getting up close to the house, I feel a little intimidated. It looks so grand. I pull my dress down a little and nervously fix my hair again after I press the doorbell.

"Mia!" Elle greets me warmly as the door swings open and she gestures me straight in. "You're just in time!"

Holy shit. The inside of her house looks better than most five-star hotels I have stayed in. Everything is marble and carefully colour coordinated. It's very modern, which I didn't expect considering the outside looks more rustic.

"Thanks for inviting me over, Elle," I respond politely but I'm distracted by the spiral staircase in the background.

"House tour?" Elle offers with a laugh. I must be gawping too obviously.

"Sure," I agree with a nod.

"Great! First, let me fix you a drink. I made a few jugs of a special cocktail I like; thought you might want to try it."

I smile enthusiastically and follow behind Elle as she leads me into the kitchen. Her kitchen is probably bigger than my kitchen and lounge area combined. It's beautiful and leads straight out into her garden; I can't see it fully, but it looks as though the garden could be the size of a football field. It's phenomenal. I quickly spot their swimming pool, and a hot tub in the corner too.

"Here we are!" Elle smiles brightly as she brings two jugs of a red concoction to the kitchen island. "It's basically a sangria with a few little extras."

Elle pours a large glass and passes it to me proudly. Sangria is one of my favourite drinks, so I don't hesitate to take a gulp. It looks so refreshing.

"Jesus…" I cough. It's a lot stronger than I anticipated; the sharp kick has hit the back of my throat and I'm trying my best not to show myself up by spluttering everywhere. This isn't like a sangria I have ever tasted before.

"Ah yeah, I forgot to mention – you may want to sip it to start with, it has ouzo in it," Elle giggles.

"Ouzo?"

"Yeah. Jacob and I have been huge fans of it ever since our honeymoon in Greece. Ever been to Greece, Mia?"

"Um, no, I haven't," I respond, trying not to cough again. "Speaking of Jacob, is he not around today?"

"Yes. He's around," Elle replies but her smiley exterior switches for a more despondent reaction. "He's just in his office."

"Oh?" I smile.

"Yep. You know men. The work never stops does it?"

"I guess not." I smile agreeably and take another sip of my drink, careful not to gulp it this time.

So far, the house certainly matches Elle's personality. There are a lot of professional photos of her and Jacob hanging on the walls, and lots of them on holidays, or at the Grand National posing with jockeys and horses. Must be a hobby of theirs. It looks like they have a wonderful life and they're obviously very proud of it to have so many pictures on display.

"Oh yeah! House tour," Elle suddenly says as she jumps off the kitchen stool.

I sip my drink frequently as Elle takes me from room to room to stop me from shouting "holy shit" every time I walk into the next exquisite part of their enormous house. First, we check out the wine cellar as it's right next to the kitchen. Depressingly, the wine cellar is probably bigger than my bathroom. Don't get me wrong, I absolutely love my house, I love all the light, the glass walls and everything – but compared to this house, it looks like a bloody Travelodge.

Next we head into their gym. Not a place that impresses me much if I'm honest but it's clear Jacob uses this room a lot. At least that's what his tight white shirt led me to believe last night.

"Holy shit," I blurt as we step into the third room. "Shit. Sorry. I didn't mean to swear."

Elle just giggles and looks at me a little bemused. We have walked into what can only be described as the sports room. It has a huge white and blue felt snooker table, a dart board, a large flat-screen television with Sky Sports on, a golf simulator and a mini bar area. It's so unbelievably cool I'm lost for words. The bar area is decorated like a typical old pub you'd find in London. It's impressive.

"This is Jacob's room," Elle sighs as she rolls her eyes. "Unfortunately, I had no say in the decor."

"Oh, I didn't say holy shit because of the decor," I stutter. "I'm a sports journalist. I love sports. This is right up my street."

"Oh?" Elle reacts so quietly I barely hear her.

"Yep. I know, it's not very girly but it's just always been my thing. This is insanely cool. I love it!" I beam as I study the cabinet of sports memorabilia and old trophies which I assume belong to Jacob.

I notice Elle seems a little unimpressed as she watches me . I get the feeling I have somehow disappointed her by telling her what I do for a living.

"I hate sports," she eventually groans. "It's a bugbear of Jacob's that I don't enjoy any of that. But I personally think it's all such a waste of time."

"Oh? But I saw your photos at the Grand National?"

"Oh! That!" Elle bursts with an exaggerated loud laugh. "Darling, I just like to dress up! I couldn't care less about the horses. Anyway, let's move on."

With that she turns on her heel and marches out of what is clearly her least favourite room in the house and we begin to head on up the stairs.

As I carefully climb the spiral staircase, I see more and more photos of her and Jacob along the wall. At first, it was quite endearing and cute but now it reminds me of an old *OK!* magazine from the late nineties and I feel like I'm seeing every picture from a cheesy photo collection of Posh and Becks.

"Darling, you'll love this room." Elle smiles confidently as we head into a white room. Everything is white. The carpets, the chaise longue, the flowers, the drapes, the cushions, everything.

"Wow," I react politely, although I'm not sure what I am supposed to be excited about. It is essentially a giant walk-in wardrobe. It probably is every little girls' dream to be fair, but I was much more in my element downstairs in the sports room.

"Here, I have all my amazing limited-edition collections and prize pieces. Take this for example, this entire wardrobe contains all my bags, from Louis Vuitton to Birkin." She boastfully gestures to one of three walk-in wardrobes.

"Then here, we have shoes! I love my shoes. We have Jimmy Choo, Gucci, Roger Vivier, Dolce and Gabbana. The usual."

"Impressive." I smile.

"Who's your favourite shoe designer Mia?" Elle questions me eagerly.

"Um…well. I like lots really. All kinds," I say hesitantly. Suddenly I'm very aware that my back is sweating a little bit. Why have I suddenly come over all nervous and anxious? I knew Elle was exuberant and well off, but I didn't think I would feel this intimidated by it.

"So, who?" Elle pushes.

"Um…well I quite like, err, Dune," I finally mumble.

"Ah. I haven't heard of Dune. Oh well. Let's continue with the tour, shall we?"

I nod and smile but inside I suddenly feel inferior and not quite the Mia I was twenty minutes ago when I was admiring my reflection and feeling full of confidence. I like Elle, she's wonderfully graceful and polite, but I wonder if she often makes remarks which could make people feel as if they're beneath her.

"Your home is beautiful," I offer sincerely.

"Yes. I'm very proud of it, Mia. Thank you. Jacob and I have worked so hard to get where we are today."

I take a few larger sips of my sangria. I notice I have nearly drunk it already and my head feels a little light. I didn't mean to drink it so fast, but I think Elle makes me quite nervous. The more I'm following her around this beautiful house like some kind of fan girl, the more I feel out of place.

"Ah, sounds like Jacob has jumped in the shower so I can't show you our room or our bathroom. Which is a shame because the bathroom has a steam room and a sauna in it. It really is quite amazing. I'll show you another time. There's nothing much left to show you now apart from Jacob's office, which is quite underwhelming," she jokes as she leads me into the last room at the end of the long hallway.

The first thing I notice are the bachelor's degrees framed on the walls and a few other acknowledgments.

"Wait…does that say Jackson and Shaw Solicitors?"

"Yes. That's my husband's company, he shares it with his half-brother," Elle confirms.

Jesus. Jackson and Shaw Solicitors are one of the most prestigious law firms in London. The majority of the athletes I have ever met are represented by them. Elle isn't just wealthy, she's insanely rich.

"That's incredible. I know a lot about them. They're brilliant. I was fascinated last year when I followed the Klein vs Bates case and..."

"I don't really pay much attention to Jacob's work," Elle interrupts.

"Oh. Well your husband is incredibly good at his job. If you don't mind me saying." I smile politely.

Elle forces a smile before heading out of the room. Just before I follow her, I notice something surprising. Something I didn't notice from my house. I can see my bedroom from Jacob's office. I can't see right into my room now because my sheer drapes are closed, and they allow just enough privacy. But if they were open, I'm sure you could see into my room quite clearly. Maybe it's not quite as secluded as I thought.

I keep my little discovery to myself and follow Elle out of the room and back downstairs. She ushers me out into the garden and invites me to sit at the elegantly laid table whilst she brings out another jug of sangria. I must start to pace myself now.

Chapter six

I've nearly finished my second ouzo sangria when Jacob finally makes his appearance. I get the vibe that Elle and Jacob have had some kind of marital spat because she doesn't look particularly thrilled to see him and he doesn't exactly sit next to her with much enthusiasm either.

"Mia." Jacob smiles as he pours himself a glass of the sangria. "I assume Elle has already forced you on a house tour."

"Excuse me!" Elle scoffs as she tries to laugh it off, but she looks mildly offended. "Mia was the one who wanted to look around, isn't that right Mia?"

I nod awkwardly and take the last gulp of my sangria.

"Here," Jacob says and politely refills my glass. "So, let me guess, your favourite room is the walk-in wardrobe, the room that is home to hundreds of designer labels. Every girls' dream, right?"

He looks up at me in a dismissive manner and awaits my answer as if I'm going to giggle like some airhead and agree that the shallow vanity room is the best thing I have seen in his overstated house.

I'm really starting to feel as though I don't fit in here. Jacob is an arse if he thinks he can't take me seriously because I'm a woman.

"Actually, Mia liked your sports room the most. She does some sort of blog or something to do with sports," Elle answers for me. Although she answers it in a dismissive way that makes me want to throat punch her but as usual, I smile and take Elle's rudeness as a joke.

"No, it's nothing to do with blogging. I'm a sports journalist, I run my own columns for *The British Telegraph*," I announce proudly.

Jacob's sarcastic expression drops instantly, and he looks at me with new interest. Almost as if he is impressed.

"I love that column. You're Mia Johnson?" Jacob asks eagerly as he sits up in his chair and finally decides I'm worth listening to.

"That's me!" I smile. "I'm actually quite the fan of yours too. I realised today that you're the CEO of Jackson and Shaw. I religiously read *Law Today* magazine and the article about the Klein case absolutely fascinated me. I had a feeling he was innocent but nobody else believed me; when I read what you did for him, to prove his innocence, well it was just heart-warming," I explain sincerely. I notice how Jacob's expression softens as he listens to me. He makes me quite nervous, but it feels good to have finally made a connection with at least one of my neighbours.

"Yes, it's fantastic. You're a fan of Jacob Jackson and he's a fan of some sports thing," Elle cuts in. "But let's please discuss something a little less professional and boring! I want to hear more personal things; I want to get to know the real Mia." I immediately notice Jacob's annoyance as Elle forces us to change the subject and although I keep my expression neutral, I feel the same way.

"Well, what do you want to know?" I smile and take a sip of the sangria Jacob has poured me.

"Married? Kids? Is there a famous athlete toy boy in your life? Maybe some twenty-year-old footballer?" Elle playfully winks at me.

"Err. No kids," I apprehensively start with. "And I was married.

But my divorce finalised just recently. Although we have been separated for nearly a year now."

Elle's face falls as if I have just announced something extremely depressing and catastrophic.

"Oh Mia. Couldn't you make it work?" she asks sympathetically.

"Sometimes in life it gets to the point where you don't want to keep compromising your own happiness to make something work."

Jacob smiles and nods at my explanation.

"I'm a great believer that love and relationships shouldn't be forced. It's better this way."

"I disagree. Marriage is forever. Love isn't always everything, it's also about finding someone you are most compatible with in life. That's why Jacob and I work so well together."

Jacob's expression is hard to read right now. I desperately want to hear his opinion, but I assume he shares the same views as his wife.

"Alex and I took our marriage as far as we could. But when his career came to an end, nothing I did made him enjoy our life anymore. He spiralled out of control and before I knew it, I was living with an alcoholic who seemed to hate me. Marriage can't be forever if you're going to bed every night crying yourself to sleep because you're scared of the monster your husband is becoming. Marriage can't be forever if the man who vowed to love and protect you is the same man who breaks your belongings and then raises his fist to you because he blames you for every bad thing that has happened in his life..."

My throat is a growing thick and I realise I have gotten emotional. Panicked, I look up to see Elle gawping at me. The sangria is most definitely to blame for my oversharing.

"Sorry," I sigh, full of embarrassment. "I didn't mean to tell you my life story."

Elle just smiles gleefully. "Don't be! That was the best gossip I have heard in ages."

"Did you call the police, or take legal action?" Jacob questions me assertively.

His question takes me by surprise a little bit. Maybe it's just a habit to be in lawyer mode. He probably can't help it, it's who he is.

"No, nothing like that. I left the home and we divorced," I answer a little timidly.

"So, this man smashed up your home in front of you and then threatened to assault you and you did nothing? Don't you want to protect yourself? What if he comes by your new house?" Jacob questions me with more intensity.

"He doesn't know where I live."

"It's not exactly hard to find out where people live these days Mia. You must know that, you're a smart woman."

"He isn't that type of guy. He barely leaves the house. He'll be wallowing in self-pity. He has made mistakes and I'm sure he will make more, but he isn't violent. Not like that. He has never hurt me."

"Well where I come from, a man doesn't raise a hand to a woman if he has no intention of hurting her."

"Okay!" Elle nudges Jacob. "Chill out, darling. Mia is a big girl; I think she knows what she's doing."

Jacob's eyes stay fixated on mine for a few more seconds before looking down and staring at his drink. He clenches his jaw as if he is wound up, but he doesn't say any more about it.

"Honestly Mia, sometimes I think he is incapable of talking to people like a normal human and not some hotshot lawyer."

"It's fine," I say softly and force a smile. "I appreciate the concern."

"You'll have to excuse me ladies," Jacob announces as he stands up from the table. "But I have work to do and I really shouldn't leave it any longer. It was a pleasure Mia."

Jacob turns to give Elle a kiss on the cheek before promptly disappearing back into the house.

That was weird. Since being here it feels as though Jacob has gone from writing me off as some bimbo, then growing to like me, then even caring about me and now he has walked off like he is mad at me. I can't figure him out at all. I thought I could but now I'm just confused. I really don't know if I am liked here. Elle is nice enough, but I know she thinks I am beneath her and I'm pretty sure my job is utterly ridiculous to her.

"Men!" Elle says as she playfully rolls her eyes.

I smile awkwardly and sip at my drink.

"Right, I can't be bothered with a barbecue now. Shall we order a pizza and get pissed?" Elle offers with a bright smile.

Finally, Elle has said something I can totally get on board with.

"Sure!" I say as we both gulp our drinks and giggle like two teenagers.

Wow, Elle definitely does loosen up a little after a few drinks. She's a lot more down to earth.

Three more drinks and half a Hawaiian pizza later, I'm definitely feeling tipsy. Every time I begin to make my excuses to head home, Elle pours me another drink and continues telling me about her social life and how she went to Paris Fashion Week last year and how she met Vivienne Westwood. She tells me every detail with such energy and enthusiasm. It's not usually something I would find particularly interesting, but I get lost in her storytelling. It's quite fascinating hearing how the other half live. I soon learn that Elle doesn't work, nor has she ever had a job. She has come from money and married into money and that seems to be enough for her. A housewife and a lady of leisure. Personally, I'd be bored but she makes it sound like there's never a dull moment.

I begin to realise that it's getting dark when all the solar lights come on. It's still warm though and very pleasant sitting here in their beautiful garden.

"Is it me, or are those solar lights causing double vision?" Elle slurs before throwing her head back and giggling.

I turn around and try to focus on the solar lights; they're not quite double vision but they are certainly blurry. I giggle with Elle and nod in agreement.

"I must use your bathroom, if that's okay," I say as I carefully get to my feet and steady my balance.

"Of course, darling! Oh, but use my bathroom upstairs, it has some new hand soaps from Harrods, you'll love them!" Elle calls after me as I carefully approach the house. It's quite dark outside now and my balance definitely isn't good anymore. I'm still not sure what ouzo is, but I know it's incredibly strong.

Elle wasn't wrong about her bathroom, it is very luxurious, and she's right, the hand soaps are cute. They're shaped like flowers and smell divine. I could never be as organised as Elle is, everything in her home is special. She has such an eye for detail with every little thing. I'm far too lazy to achieve that level of commitment. My reflection in the mirror tells me it's definitely time to go home. My mascara has smudged a little and my cheeks are all red, the usual colour they turn when I've had a few too many. I decide I best go out and tell Elle that I really need to get home now. After a bumpy start, I have had fun.

"Is my wife trashed yet?" Jacob startles me by saying from the doorway of his office.

"Oh! You made me jump." I giggle as I focus on his masculine figure in front of me. He's changed out of his clothing from earlier and much to my surprise is dressed very informally. Light grey tracksuit bottoms and just a short-sleeved white t-shirt.

Shit. He has tattoos all down his left arm. A whole sleeve in fact. I never noticed that before, but then again, he was wearing a formal work shirt. I would have never imagined in a million years that Jacob would be the type to have tattoos like this.

"Erm, yeah, she's a little drunk."

"And you?" he asks.

"I'm a little tipsy, yes. I'll probably head home now anyway. I'm kind of tired."

"Look, I might have spoken out of turn earlier. Your divorce isn't my business."

"Okay. Don't worry," I say so quietly it comes out as a whisper.

"But on the off chance he comes around and causes you any problems, I'm here," Jacob says authoritatively as he takes a few steps towards me, closing the gap in between us.

My heart quickens as he towers over me. I can't deny that Jacob is attractive but I'm doing my best not to pay too much attention to those thoughts. He is my neighbour, nothing more and nothing less.

I try to say thank you but for some reason the words won't come out. I notice my breathing is faster and Jacob is staring down at me intently; it makes me nervous but at the same time I feel something exciting. He stares at me as if I'm intriguing him. Like a difficult riddle that he wants to figure out.

I look up to stare at his lips quickly before meeting his eyes.

"Goodnight then, Mia," he eventually says, so casually, before putting his hands in his pockets and strolling off into his bedroom. Leaving me to catch my breath in his hallway.

Jesus, what was that? Pull yourself together Mia. I think the sangria has hit me harder than I thought.

When I get back outside, Elle has fallen asleep on her sun lounger. I decide it's best not to wake her and instead I grab my phone and quickly make my way out of the front door.

This time though, the fresh air has hit me differently. I feel quite light on my feet and I'm stumbling a little as I make my way across the road and approach my own front door.

I have a feeling I'm going to have a huge headache tomorrow.

Chapter seven

Throb. Throb. Throb. Is it normal to feel your pulse in your head and ears? Jesus, I haven't been this hungover in a long time. Mental note: maybe ask what ouzo actually is before sipping away at it and grinning like a Cheshire Cat when offered more. I can't even seem to get a clear answer from Google. It's basically some strong shit from Greece.

I squint through one eye, trying to focus on my phone. Eurgh. It's too bright. Everything hurts. I'm going back to sleep. I literally don't want to wake up until this hangover is gone. Actually first, I need to drink a bucket of water because my mouth is dry and feels like cotton. But then, I'm sleeping this off.

Knock knock. "Mia...?"

What in the world? Is that...is that Elle?

I reluctantly drag myself from the bed and carefully use my hands against the wall to steady myself as I shuffle out of my bedroom and down the stairs. My hair is a mess, my eyes are puffy, and my mouth is painfully dry. I feel like Billy from *Hocus Pocus* when he is brought back to life from his grave after a hundred years.

"Elle?" I manage to croak. The sunlight hits my eyes straightaway which makes me squint and try to shield the brightness with my hand, but I can just about make out Elle. She looks like she's ready for a day at the races. Dressed in a blue midi tight dress with her red curled locks all neatly styled to one side.

"Morning Mia." She smiles, annoyingly perky.

"Shitting hell, Elle. Where did you go to school? Xavier's school for gifted youngsters?"

"Huh?"

"Well look at you. You look...like you've been at a spa weekend. How do you do it? Weren't you drunk last night? When I left your house, you were asleep on a sun lounger with a straw hanging out of your mouth – and now look at you. You look totally unaffected. You have got to be at least part mutant?"

"Oh Mia!" Elle giggles as she tosses her hair back from her face. "You do make me laugh. But no, I just don't get hangovers much. Oh? You poor thing, are you hungover?"

A part of me wants to lie and pretend that I'm completely fine too but I think the fact that I look like I've caught the plague and I've also just noticed that one boob is hanging out of my bra makes it obvious that I really am not okay. I cover myself up with my dressing gown in the hope that Elle hasn't noticed.

"Just a little headache, yeah. But I'll be fine in a few hours," I answer casually, trying to play down the fact that my head is spinning, and I feel like I could fall over at any second.

"Okay, good. I'd hate to think my special cocktails made you poorly. Anyway, you left your purse at the house, so I thought I'd better return it."

"Oh! Thank you so much. I'd been looking for it all morning." Which is a barefaced lie. I hadn't even realised it was missing but I don't want to sound like a complete disaster.

"Well I best be off; I'm having afternoon tea with some friends. Maybe we could do drinks again soon, yes?"

"Sure," I answer politely. "Maybe you and Jacob could come over here next time?"

"Yes. We'd like that. Thank you, Mia, it's so nice to have a friend in the area," Elle replies confidently before spinning around and heading towards her black Range Rover. Of course, it has tinted windows and a personalised number plate. Elle certainly likes to make a statement wherever she can.

I close the front door behind her, grab a bottle of water out of the fridge and head straight back up to bed. I'm hoping the next time I open my eyes; I'm feeling a lot more human than I am now.

Somehow, I manage to sleep through the majority of the day and by the time I open my eyes again and glance at the clock on my bedside table I can see it's nearly five o'clock in the afternoon. Wow, I can't remember the last time I slept all day. Probably back when I was at university. I feel a lot better, but I know my chances of sleeping tonight now are very low.

Although I physically feel a lot better, I can't help noticing that I have woken up feeling low. I'm not sure why, but I just know that I'm feeling quite sorry for myself. To be fair it's probably the alcohol from last night that's done it. They do say that alcohol is a depressant and it always seems to be the case with me. In the past, I have often woken up feeling a little sad and vulnerable after a heavy night. Right now, I feel lonely. For the first time in a year I feel very...single.

I decide to run myself a bath and have a long soak. I light some candles and put my old record player on. I picked it up at a local market back when I was living in London and although I don't have a lot of records to play on it, I absolutely love it. It's so vintage and classy. I let Cher's album play quietly in the background whilst I unwind in the bath. Another little bargain I had picked up from the market that day.

My mind starts wandering back to last night. It was mostly

fun; I think I like Elle. She can be a great laugh, although naturally she's a little eccentric. I'm not sure how I feel about Jacob. He seems a little distant and moody; he prejudged me – it was only when I told him that I'm a journalist that he eased up and seemed to take me seriously. Which makes me wonder if he would take me seriously if I just worked in the grocery shop around the corner. Is he a little pretentious like Elle? I'm not sure. But my god he is gorgeous! I almost feel embarrassed at the realisation I'm sitting here thinking this about my neighbour. Thinking how pathetic and needy it is to be lusting after some married man. I'm not really, I mean I hardly know him. I don't know why my heart raced when he came so close to me and stood over me the way he did, it's likely it was just because I was far too tipsy for my own good. But I can't deny that he is attractive.

The thought fades from my mind just as quickly as it entered it. There's no point thinking this way. Instead, I think my evening will be filled with three other men instead: Ben & Jerry and a certain Mr Grey.

When I climb out of the bath and go back into my bedroom, I notice Elle's car still isn't back so I'm guessing afternoon tea is running over for her. I roll my eyes at the thought of posh women sitting around a grand table whilst stuffing their faces with overpriced cucumber sandwiches and cakes. Wow, maybe now I'm the one who is judging.

As I rummage through my underwear drawer, I find a little white lace night dress I had gotten from a sale a few months ago. I reach for it and pull it over my head and over my body. I instantly like the way it feels and when I glance at myself in the mirror, I'm excited by how sexy it makes me look. I needed this little pick me up. It encourages me to go the full hog and give myself a little spruce, so I apply some gradual tanning moisturiser over my body and when that's finished, I give my hair a proper blow dry, which leaves it feeling soft and bouncy. My pamper has made me feel quite a bit better. I bring in the candles from the bathroom and place them on my bedside table and put *Fifty Shades of Grey* into the DVD player.

I'm lying on my front, comfortably stretched out whilst digging into my ice cream and enjoying watching Jamie Dornan on my screen when I'm suddenly distracted by a light shining into my bedroom windows. It's Jacob's office light. I hadn't noticed it was so bright before. When I peer up, I see him standing by his desk and sorting through papers. Poor guy never seems to stop working. Then I notice something I had forgotten about. Tattoos all down one arm. I remember I saw them last night; I remember because it surprised me then too. They don't seem to match the professional man he presents as. He isn't wearing a top, only light grey joggers.

His body is masculine and defined. I might be across the street, but I can tell quite well that he is toned and muscular. My heartbeat quickens again, and I notice I'm breathing more heavily.

God Mia, snap out of it. He's just a neighbour and you're just very single and bored, I tell myself.

I'm probably just missing a man's touch and it has nothing directly to do with Jacob. I don't think.

I look away and try to concentrate on the movie, but my eyes keep gazing back out of my window and across to Jacob's office. I'm drawn in like a moth to a flame and as much as I tell myself this is silly; I can't stop myself from watching him and I like it.

Without thinking, I turn the television off and now my room is only lit up by the candles. I slowly walk over to my windows and get a closer look at Jacob. I study his body, his arms, his broad shoulders, the slight curve in his lower back. I almost like the fact I can see him, and he doesn't know. My breathing is faster, and the more I watch him, the more intense I feel.

I tuck my hair behind my ear and as my hand leaves my face, I allow it to stroke gently over my chest and feel my hardened nipples through the lace fabric.

Shit. I'm so lost in my private little moment that I'm startled when I look back up to Jacob's face and see him staring directly back at me. Fuck. What do I do? I could play it down and walk away from the window as if it was an innocent glance over. I could play it down. I should. But I'm already reaching for the strap on my night dress and I'm pulling it down over my shoulders. He doesn't turn away. He watches. So, I slowly pull at the other strap and let it fall down, revealing my breasts to him.

My heart pounds. I shouldn't feel this turned on, but I do. Jacob sits perched against his desk with his hands down, gripping the desk either side of him and he is watching me. He is fixated on me.

I let the dress fall lower until eventually it sits over my feet. I have nothing on now but the white lace thong that came with the dress. I glance down at my body before looking back for his reaction. To my surprise and excitement, he starts untying the string to his joggers, revealing the bulge in his black briefs. He pulls his joggers off before perching back against his desk. His thighs are thick and all I can think about is how desperately I want to be in between them.

His focus is back on me as if he is waiting for my next move.

I have no idea what I'm doing or what I'm thinking. I'm not even sure how far I am willing to take this but all I know is that I can't stop. I can feel myself throbbing inside my underwear and I need to be touched.

Whilst keeping my eyes locked on Jacob's, I slowly bring my hand over the thin lace that barely covers me, and I stroke slowly across the most sensitive area. I let out a sigh and bite my bottom lip as I feel myself pulsating.

All I can think about right now is how much I want Jacob inside of me.

I take a step back and lean on the edge of my bed. I arch my back and pant harder as my strokes get faster. When I look back towards Jacob, he is off his desk and leaning against his office window, watching me with more intensity.

I can already feel the pressure building. I can't believe what I'm doing but I'm too excited to stop. All I can think about now are Jacob's eyes watching me, watching me pleasure myself and my god it feels good. I'm enjoying every second of this little show I am putting on for him. With my spare hand I start cupping at my breasts and I start rocking my hips against my fingers. I feel so sexy right now, so powerful. I'm showing Jacob something I know he wants.

When I stare back up to see Jacob's response, he is frantically pulling up his joggers. I stop touching myself immediately and curiously watch him. Why has he stopped?

Without looking back, he darts out of his office. The office light is switched off and my bedroom is suddenly darker.

I hold my breath a little, wondering if he is about to walk across the street and through my front door.

I wonder if he is going to come charging up my stairs and throw me down onto my bed and give me the most passionate sex I have ever had.

Shit. His front door has flown open and I see him making his way down the path. This is it.

But before I can allow myself to get any more excited, I watch him climb into his car instead. Within a second, he starts up the car and heads out of his driveway and out of our street.

Oh god. What *have* I done? Where has he gone? What if he tells

Elle? Shit, *Elle.*

Chapter eight

The heat from the water beats down on my back; it hurts but I do nothing about it. I sit huddled on the floor of my shower with my knees tucked up against my chest, allowing the hot water to wash away my guilt. Well, at least I hope that's what it'll do. How could I be so stupid?

I have been married, I have taken the vows, I understand the sanctity of marriage and yet I have given in to some stupid temptation and massively let myself down.

I cringe at the flashbacks of the woman I was just moments ago, taking off my night dress in front of Jacob in the seductive way I did. I am pathetic. Where did I honestly think this was going to go? What did I expect to gain from it?

I am so embarrassed and all I can think about is Elle and what if Jacob tells her. He probably will, she's his wife, he will probably want to come clean; he'll tell her how I was trying to arouse him through a fucking window. She'll hate me, then word will spread, and my little neighbourhood will all think I'm some disgusting homewrecker.

I'm so mad at my actions, it's almost as if I'm punishing myself by continuing to let the hot water sting my back.

I felt something with Jacob though, a spark of some kind. He made my heart race. Each time he looked at me I felt completely captivated by him, every time he asked me a question last night, I just wanted my answer to be good enough to impress him. I haven't felt like that before, not even with Alex.

The thought doesn't make me feel much better though; it's no justification and I still majorly overstepped a line. I can't even believe I did it. In my whole life, I have never done something like that with such confidence and provocativeness. It's a side of me I didn't even realise I had. I don't know what came over me. I really don't, but I know I need to fix it, somehow.

By the time I finally manage to pick myself up from the shower floor, I notice its nearly midnight and oddly Jacob's car still isn't back in the driveway where it usually is. I can't see Elle's car either.

I stare curiously at their house – there's no sign of life at all. I wonder what has happened. I have to actively stop my mind from racing wildly to reasons why he might have rushed off like that. I don't want to worry myself even more, I'm already starting to feel sick.

I lost myself in that moment but now I'm back in reality and my reality is that I'm single, he is successful, married to a beautiful woman in a fabulous home and I'm just me, newly divorced, lonely, pathetic and spending my evenings talking to the local stray cat. All I want to do now is switch off and fall asleep, but my long nap earlier has prevented any chances of that.

Instead I sit by my bedroom window with a glass of wine and just wallow in the dark, feeling sorry for myself. The wine goes down nicely. I tell myself I'm not drinking to numb the embarrassment of tonight's antics, but I think it's clear from how quickly I'm knocking them back that I'm on a mission. I just want to feel good again and not like this.

As I swallow the last mouthful of wine from my fourth glass, I notice headlights appearing out of the corner of my eye. It's Jacob's car, he's back. I stare eagerly through the gap in my drapes as I desperately try to learn what could have happened. I'm half wondering if Elle is about to come storming over the road and bang on my door, although she doesn't seem the type to be fair. She's probably far too elegant to engage in some public slanging match in the street.

What the...?

Jacob is pulling Elle out of the backseat and carrying her from the car. She looks asleep or passed out. It's hard to tell and it's dark so I can't make out anything specific, but her hair is a mess and one of her shoes is missing. She definitely doesn't look like she did when I last saw her.

I wait anxiously and pace around my bedroom. I'm not sure what I'm waiting for. I guess I'm hoping Jacob will turn up and we'll just laugh it all off and I'll ask if Elle is okay and I'll offer to help and try to be a good friend, and everything will be fine.

But the more time goes on, the more anxious I get. I can't see much movement coming from across the street and definitely no sign of Jacob making his way to my door.

I can't leave it like this. I'm not sure if it's my nerves or the wine but I'm shoving my sliders on and throwing a dressing gown over my shoulders and making my way down the stairs.

I can't just sit and do nothing. I can't just wait and see if this is going to blow up in my face; the whole thing makes me feel sick. I can try and nip this in the bud now and we can all forget it ever happened.

I almost tiptoe as I approach their front door, which I notice immediately has been left ajar. It's too late to knock, I don't want to wake Elle if she's unwell. Perhaps I'll just walk in and hover in the hallway until Jacob appears.

I quietly step inside, but it's dark and I can barely gather my bearings. The lights are off, apart from a glow streaming from underneath the door of the sports room.

What the hell am I doing here?

Half of me thinks I should get out now and quickly get back home before anyone notices that I'm even here. But the other half just wants to get this thing over and done with. I'm reluctant and scared but my feet are taking over and I'm walking towards the sports room anyway.

"Jacob?" I whisper as I slowly open the door.

"What the fuck, Mia?" Jacob snaps as he throws down his snooker cue on the table.

He is back to being shirtless with his light grey joggers on, but his demeanour is totally different now. He is angry and I'm sure I have just made it worse by turning up.

"I'm sorry. I didn't mean to startle you..."

"Then don't fucking walk into my house in the middle of the night!"

"I'm sorry, the door was open, I just needed to speak to you, I can leave?"

Jacob rolls his eyes and lets out a sigh.

"Just tell me what you want that's so important it couldn't wait until the morning, Mia."

I hate the way he says my name like that at the end of each sentence. It's so formal and unfriendly. Like I'm nothing but an annoyance to him.

"I just wanted to...to apologise. For earlier. I didn't mean for that to happen; I just want you to know that I'm so sorry and it won't be happening again..."

I'm suddenly so nervous I can barely find my words, and Jacob's sharp stare only makes me more jittery.

"I didn't know you were watching; I mean, I didn't realise you could see me..."

"Bullshit," Jacob scoffs. "You really want to play that game, do you Mia? You want to pretend you weren't loving every single moment that my eyes were all over you whilst you touched yourself?"

The bluntness in his words makes me feel more embarrassed than ever before.

"I... I don't know, can we just forget the whole thing?" I stutter anxiously, barely making eye contact anymore.

"Relax. I won't be telling Elle a thing. It'll only make her worse."

"Worse?" I ask curiously.

"Forget it," Jacob snaps back impatiently.

Jacob picks up his snooker cue and hovers over the table as he hits a ball and I watch it slide into the pocket.

"Is she okay?" I whisper. "I saw her earlier and she seemed fine, you know, considering we had quite a bit to drink last night; she didn't even seem hungover."

"Well she wouldn't, because she doesn't get hangovers. She's not usually sober long enough to get them. Most people wake up to a cup of coffee in the morning, my wife wakes up and has a few shots of vodka before she even gets in the shower, so that's why she looked fine, Mia."

"Oh...I had no idea, she seems so..."

"Yeah well, you wouldn't have any idea, would you? You're too busy acting like a slapper and getting naked at your fucking bedroom window for your married neighbour to see. Meanwhile my wife was out drinking herself to death. I can't be distracted by you Mia. Some of us have fucking responsibilities that we can't just ignore for a night," Jacob roars, stepping bullishly towards me which frightens me a little.

The harshness of his insults hurt, and I can feel myself getting upset. I try desperately to hold my emotions back, but I know the tears are filling my eyes.

"I won't bother you again," I manage to say through the lump in my throat and I immediately rush out of the room as quickly as I can.

Before I reach the front door, I'm startled by an almighty crashing noise. It sounds like Jacob has punched the door, but I can't be sure. I pick up the pace until I'm practically running back home, my heart pounding and my bottom lip quivering. My stomach is in knots and I'm holding my breath to stop myself from sobbing. The second I am back inside my home I lock the front door behind me and fall to a heap on the floor and finally give into the tears.

I am humiliated. The word *slapper* keeps popping into my mind. The sharpness of his tongue when he said it shows what he thinks of me and that's all I need to know. How did things get so out of control?

Chapter nine

The day seems to have flown by. I got up early, got myself dressed, got settled in the office and threw myself into my work. I even started preparing some columns for next week too. It was a welcome relief to have my work to concentrate on, it took my mind off last night.

I have decided that I'm not going to allow myself to be upset anymore. I made a mistake – turns out I'm not as perfect as I thought, but I am a good person and I don't deserve to be called a slapper by Jacob. He watched me, that must mean something. So, there's no way I can allow his insult to have any merit. I'm single, I'm not being unfaithful to anyone. He should really look in the mirror before he starts name calling.

I have spent the last eighteen months trying to build my confidence back up and I am sure as hell not going to let Jacob Jackson knock it down. I said sorry, I tried to make things right and he didn't want to do anything other than call me names. I'm not going to dwell. I shall just keep my distance as much as I can and let Elle and me naturally drift apart, that way nobody has to get hurt.

I scrape my hair up into a top knot and throw on some comfy pyjamas. Tonight, I'm going to spend my evening making fajitas and then maybe a homemade cheesecake, anything to keep my mind occupied.

"Puss!" I squeal a little too excitedly as I see the beautiful grey cat waiting for me by the patio doors again. I instantly slide the doors open and let her come running in. I love her company; she makes me feel a little less lonely in this house. She purrs heavily as she makes herself comfortable on my sofa and I can't help but smile.

"Make yourself comfy, Puss," I giggle to myself. I'm very aware this is crazy cat lady territory but I'm in far too deep now to stop it. I may as well embrace it: "My name is Mia and my only friend in the suburbs is Puss, the stray neighbourhood cat!"

"Mia! Darling?" I hear Elle call from the front door.

Oh god, Elle.

I can tell from her voice that she is clueless about last night. Jacob did say he wouldn't burden her with it, but my hands are suddenly sweating anyway.

"Coming!" I call back, trying to sound as friendly and as upbeat as possible.

As soon as I open the door I'm met with Elle's big smile as she waves sangria in front of my face. Jesus, please, no more alcohol. I don't think I can stomach any more.

"Sangria time!" she cheers excitedly. "Oh wow, Mia, something smells delicious."

I try to appear as nonchalant as possible, but every time she looks at me, I keep panicking that somehow my face will tell her everything that happened.

"Oh, I'm just making some fajitas, would you like some?"

"I'd love some! Grab me a glass darling and I'll pour you some of my famous sangria," she says with a wink.

I feel myself relaxing a little, it's not as awkward as I feared. She clearly has no idea about my stupid moment of madness and as long as Jacob doesn't tell her, then everything can just stay the same.

"And who is this cutie pie?" Elle asks as she perches next to Puss.

"Oh." I laugh. "It seems I have adopted a cat. She came by the night I moved in and she seems to be dropping by regularly ever since."

"Oh, that is adorable! She obviously loves your company, Mia."

"I really like hers too," I say.

Elle throws back a sangria quite quickly and fills herself another glass. Now that I know she has a problem with her drink I just feel sad watching her. The other night was fun, but that's when I thought it was a one-off.

"Was everything okay last night Elle? I noticed you still weren't back when I went to bed," I curiously ask, bending the truth.

"Oh, yeah, that." Elle looks up slightly flustered. "A friend needed me, she's been going through a tough time and so I went back to her house. I drank a bit too much though and my friend called Jacob to come and get me so that I didn't get back in my car, that was it really. So yeah, I ended up being quite late."

"Ah, I see. Sorry to hear about your friend, I hope she's okay?"

"She's fine. It's just marital problems, no big deal. We all have them. You should know that more than most, you're divorced already," she says quite harshly.

I awkwardly look down at the pan and pretend to be so busy stirring the chicken that I didn't hear her properly.

"Shit, Mia, I'm sorry. I'm feeling a little stressed out myself lately. I won't bore you with it though."

The need to know what is going on with Jacob and Elle takes over me. I'm eager to know why Jacob seems so unhappy and

Elle drinks the way she does. I don't know how far I can push it, but I know that Elle becomes a lot chattier after a few drinks. I serve up our fajitas and sit back whilst she takes drink after drink, waiting for the right time to ask her again.

"These fajitas are gorgeous!" Elle smiles as she takes another bite. "But I'm so full I couldn't possibly eat another thing. I'll stick with the sangria if you don't mind."

"Of course not." I smile back.

"Oh, I almost forgot! It's my birthday on Saturday and I'm having a house party, it's *Great Gatsby* themed! I know it's short notice, but would you like to come?"

"I'd absolutely love to, I'm sure I can whip up a costume within the next few days."

"Great! I can't wait for you to meet my friends, you'll love them. They're just like me."

"Brilliant," I respond with a bright smile but in my mind that brilliant sounds a lot more sarcastic.

"Shit. I'm all out of sangria. Well I guess that's a sign I should be going."

"No, wait...I have a bottle of red I've been waiting to open; fancy a glass?"

Oh great, good one Mia. Supply the alcoholic with more booze just to squeeze her for some answers. That's really sane Mia, I think to myself. Although, let's face it, it's not the craziest thing I've done in the last couple of days.

Elle's face lights up at the mention of the wine and she nods her head enthusiastically. I grab the bottle from the cabinet and fill her glass to the brim.

"You know Elle..." I begin as she takes a gulp of her wine. "As someone who has been divorced, I'm a pretty good listener when it comes to marital problems. I'm here if you ever want to talk about anything."

"You think you can offer me advice?" Elle smirks.

"I don't know, but I could try."

"Okay Mia...what would you do if your best friend told you she fucked your husband?"

"I... what?"

"Thought so!" Elle giggles before taking another mouthful of her wine.

Jacob cheated? I mean, I can't say I'm surprised considering he was more than happy to watch me last night, but he actually cheated? He actually fucking cheated. Why am I so angry about this?

"Scumbag," I hiss under my breath.

Shit. I was supposed to say that in my head.

"Sorry Elle! I didn't mean..."

"No, it's fine! He was a scumbag for that. But I forgave him, and I forgave my best friend too."

"Wow? Your best friend?"

"Yes." Elle sighs heavily as she recalls the incident. "I've known her my entire life, she's like a sister. Her husband had not long died, he was involved in a hit and run. She had been a mess since the second she learned of his death. She got herself in a state, drank too much, even got herself addicted to prescription pills. One night, she wouldn't answer her phone and I had gotten worried about her. I sent Jacob out to find her and he said he found her in some bar. The next thing I know, my best friend turns up at my house a few days later, crying, telling me all about how she screwed my husband in the back of his car."

Scumbag. Scumbag. Scumbag. Why am I so fucking angry? I feel like someone has just kicked me in the stomach and he isn't even my husband. He hasn't even betrayed me.

"I'm so sorry Elle, you deserve better."

"It's fine. I don't need pity. My husband made a mistake and my best friend was vulnerable, broken hearted and ridiculously drunk, she didn't know what she was doing. She's my best friend and I know she's sorry."

"Well you're a better person than I am. I probably would have slashed her tyres," I say jokingly.

"It's just a shame that my marriage still isn't on track, isn't it? It's like he didn't want to be forgiven," Elle slurs before downing her wine.

"Slow down Elle."

"He doesn't touch me anymore. We don't even sleep in the same bed. Isn't that pathetic? He usually falls asleep in his office or downstairs on the sofa. I forgave him. He should be ecstatic. Why do you think he isn't ecstatic?"

"I... I don't know. Maybe he feels like he doesn't deserve your forgiveness?"

"No, no, it's not that. It's like...it's like...oh nothing," Elle eventually huffs. She grabs the bottle from the table and fills her glass back up.

"It's like what, Elle?"

"It's like he thought it was going to be the end of our relationship and he is disappointed that it isn't."

I'm not sure what to say. Seeing Elle show me so much emotion is different, I didn't know she had it in her and yet she's spilling her heart out to me and all I can think about is how I have let her down as well. I take a sip of my drink as the guilt washes over me.

"You know what's funny? He doesn't like many people, but he seems to like you Mia. Do you know why I think that is?"

"Erm, why?"

"You're smart. You're into sports and you have a proper career. He doesn't understand that my role as a housewife is also a full-time job, so he doesn't respect it. But since you've been over, he's started rereading your columns. I even caught him googling you one night."

"Um, oh." I shift in my seat awkwardly.

I thought Elle had a glamorous job, I guess I got that wrong.

"Don't worry, he isn't a weird stalker, he was just reading up on your sports career, I guess. Sports are his passion. That's all. Well…I better head home," Elle slurs again as she stumbles to her feet.

"Woah, careful. Do you want me to walk you back?"

"Sure. If you like. I don't usually drink a lot but that red wine is strong." She giggles as she stumbles into my coffee table, knocking off some candles.

"Whoops! Sorry."

"That's fine, don't worry. Just lean on me and I'll get you home."

My heart starts racing as I approach Elle's front door. The last person I wanted to be seeing was Jacob. Elle puts her key in the lock and pushes the door open. I carefully steady Elle into the hallway; luckily, there's no sign of Jacob yet.

"Darling, could you help me up the stairs? I just need a little lie down."

"Sure, no problem," I say, and I hold onto Elle tightly as we climb the stairs.

"Here we are! My little boudoir!" Elle cheers loudly as she collapses onto her bed. "This room has seen little to no action. Zero!" she shouts before giggling to herself.

"What's going on?" Jacob suddenly appears behind me.

"I had a little drink with my friend, relax hubby!"

"I... I just thought it best I walked her home. I best be going. Bye Elle."

"Bye Mia! See you Saturday!"

"Wait!" Jacob hisses after me as I head back into the hallway.

I stop nervously as he steps close to me, forcing me to back into the wall.

"What?" I mumble.

"I tell you that my wife has a drink problem and you let her get into this state?"

"She was already quite drunk, she had sangria."

"I tipped the sangria she made away and replaced it with an alcohol-free one, so do you want to tell me how she's in this mess?" he growls through gritted teeth.

"I... I had some wine and I guess she wanted some. I'm sorry."

"I have a big day tomorrow and now I have to be up until god knows what time making sure she doesn't choke on her fucking vomit and all you have to say is sorry?"

"You know what? Your wife's mental state isn't my responsibility. Maybe she drinks so much because you fucked her best friend," I snap back, ready to storm off but his hand slams on the wall next to my face, preventing me from leaving.

"What? Did she tell you that?" he asks, looking confused and irritated.

"Yes!" I yell. "Now move your arm, I'm going home."

"Mia..." Jacob sighs before moving in even closer to me. He towers over me, keeping one arm against the wall. He lowers his neck down to look at me, pauses and then fixes on my eyes, studying me intently. I feel my heart quicken again but my head is too confused to allow myself to get lost in him this time.

"No, I'm going," I say and push hard against his chest, forcing him to take a step back.

I rush down the stairs and leave the house without looking back. This is getting too messy; I can't get too close to him. Their marital problems are nothing to do with me. I can't allow myself to get caught up in this.

Chapter ten

An hour or so later, I have managed to clean up the kitchen after the fajitas and rearrange the coffee table after Elle drunkenly fell into it. The shame of knowing I gave Elle wine knowing full well she's already having difficulties with alcohol is weighing heavily on my mind. I just wanted the ground to swallow me up when Jacob told me those sangrias, she had were virgin. I felt so stupid. I really shouldn't have done it.

I don't know what has gotten into me lately. Well actually, I do. Jacob. Ever since meeting him, I'm just not myself. Which is so out of character for me. Ever since I was a teenager, all I have ever done is followed life by the rule book. I studied hard at school, I went to one of the best universities, I worked hard for my career, I met a man and fell in love, I got married, I obsessed about my credit score, I turned a house into a home. I did all the things that I was supposed to do, and I did them well.

I had never put a toe out of line in my life. I have always considered myself to have good morals and pride myself on making good decisions, and yet here I am: stripping in front of my neighbour, getting involved in their marriage, supplying an alcoholic with more booze just so I can fulfil my own curiosity. And of course, I can't forget the fact that I talk to a cat like it's my own personal therapist.

I'm different from the person I thought I was going to be here. I thought I'd be calm, content and busy throwing myself into my work, attending local sports games, taking up yoga, going for long country walks, growing vegetables in my garden – or whatever it is people in the country do. I must have gotten to a point in my life where I was bored of playing by the rules every time. Playing it so safe and doing the right thing – where has it got me? I think a part of me is tired of being so sensible and so painfully predictable.

I let Puss out for the night and pull the sack from the kitchen bin ready to take out to the rubbish.

"Hey," Jacob says quietly as I open my front door.

"Fuck, you scared me," I gasp as I drop the bag. "I erm, I was just taking this out to the rubbish."

"Sorry...I didn't mean to scare you. I came over here to apologise."

"Oh?"

"You were right. My wife is not your responsibility. I shouldn't have pinned that on you and if I'm being completely honest, if she hadn't come here and drunk wine with you, she would only have found something stronger at home," he explains, sincerely.

I like this side of Jacob. His voice is softer, his eyes kinder and his approach to me is much gentler.

"Thank you," I mumble awkwardly.

He pauses for a moment whilst looking down at the ground and when he looks back at me, his eyes are sterner.

"Look, I don't think you should come to the party on Saturday," he says, confirming to me that his demeanour has once again changed. Once again, he changes back to serious Jacob.

"And why is that?"

"Because...because I said so. It won't be your kind of party anyway. Elle's friends are all wives of boring old rich men who think they're above everyone they meet. You'd hate it, so please, just stay home."

"Jacob, Elle invited me, and I don't want to let her down."

"God, Mia. Must you be so difficult about everything?" he snaps impatiently. "I don't want you there because I don't have time to worry about some silly crush you have on me during my wife's party. Okay? I'm sure there are other neighbours you can entertain."

And there he goes again. Back to insulting me.

"What's your problem with me?" I attempt to snap back but it comes out like more of a whine. "If it's about the other night, I said I'm sorry. Believe me, it won't happen again."

"Don't flatter yourself Mia. I haven't even thought about it since."

His words feel like they could knock the wind out of my chest. His expression is angry and impatient. Where does he get off making me feel like nothing?

"I have to go Jacob. I have a costume to sort out. Goodnight," I say as I close the door in his face.

I feel like I'm trembling, I'm so worked up. Who does he think he is? I have never known anyone to get under my skin like he does. Just when I thought he was being reasonable and genuine; he comes out with a line like that.

Just for that, I'll grab a cup of coffee, head to my office and spend some time finding the best dress for this party.

After browsing for hours through different dresses, I end up settling on the sexiest one I can find and order it for next day delivery. It's a black and gold deep plunge sequin dress, short and daring. Which to be fair, was very much the style back then. It's not at all what I had in mind originally, but I am keen to look my very best.

So clearly my plan to stay away and phase out my friendship with Elle isn't quite going to plan considering I have spent the evening online shopping for her *Great Gatsby* party. But I hated the way Jacob made me feel. He is so up and down; I'm sick of him thinking that he can talk to me how he wants. The worst part is that occasionally I feel him drawn to me, in the same way I was drawn to him last night at the window, but he'd never admit it. He would much rather tell me I'm a slapper, a forgettable one at that.

So, I suppose this dress is my way of getting back at him, looking teasingly seductive but knowing full well he can't have me. Of course, the idea sounds petty when I actually think about it, but I can't help it.

I know I'm playing with fire. I know I'm getting caught up in something I should stay away from. Every time I tell myself I'll stay away and forget about him, I find myself glancing over to his office from my window, hoping to see him.

It's like one minute I hate him but the next I'm intrigued by him. He is angry, rude, aggressive at times but when he gets close to me and focuses on my eyes, I feel myself going weak.

It's a feeling I haven't had before and it's like a drug. The more I feel it, the more I want it.

I realise how tired I am when I finally climb into bed. My eyes feel so heavy; all this stuff is a little mentally draining. It's a stress and an excitement all in one. Something I am just not used to.

Chapter eleven

The last couple of days were spent venturing back into the head office in London. It was nice to see everyone again and have a little catch up. A few friends asked to come over for an evening to see the new house and have a few drinks, which of course I would love – I miss them all a lot. The only drawback of living here is that my social life has majorly plummeted, but I still know it is the right thing for me right now. I almost missed the hustle and bustle of those busy city streets though, almost.

In all honesty, arranging to work from home part-time has been the best decision. I'll always love London, but the older I'm getting, the more impatient I am with it. The thought of sitting in traffic or commuting on busy trains with no space to sit, pushed up against someone's sweaty armpit, is far too much to bear now.

I'm quite lucky really that I have this option. I find that I work more productively from home too, I don't get caught up in office gossip or feeling forced to drown myself in coffees just to keep me alert after the draining commute. Yes, things in my work life have definitely improved.

But right now, work is the last thing on my mind as I sit here waxing my legs and preparing for Elle's party tonight. The dress arrived yesterday, and I absolutely love it, it looks even better than it did in the pictures. It was quite pricey, but it'll be worth it.

I got Elle a gift too whilst I was back in London; it was tricky finding something – I mean, what do you buy someone who already has everything? I nearly bought her a journal, I thought maybe she could use it to write down her thoughts and feelings and it may possibly help her offload some of those stresses and perhaps even help her feel a bit better so she wouldn't feel the need to drink so much. But after hesitating over it for nearly twenty minutes, I decided to put it back. I'm not close enough to her to know if she would appreciate something like that or whether she would feel patronised. Plus, I'm not sure if I can picture Elle writing much. So, I played it safe and chose a nice pamper set; I think it's a nice gift albeit quite boring. But I haven't known Elle for very long and hopefully she'll still appreciate it.

I have a quick shower to rinse off after waxing my legs and once I'm back in my bedroom, I sit and focus on my hair and make-up. I put a few loose curls through my short blonde hair and style my side fringe back to give it a bit of height. It feels very twenties and I'm proud of how well it comes out. The make-up from the twenties is probably my favourite part, the eye make-up was very dark and smoky, and it was always finished with bold red lips. I absolutely love playing around with my make-up and achieving this look. I admire my reflection in the mirror, the red lipstick is sexy and it's boosting my confidence.

I carefully take the dress from the hanger and step into it. I adjust my breasts with some tape and make sure they're sitting nicely with not too much cleavage on show. I finish my look with some black stockings, stilettos and costume jewellery.

My stomach feels as though it's doing flips, I am definitely getting nervous, but I'm determined to go and have a good time and show Jacob that I couldn't care less about him. Although one quick whiskey and diet Coke for Dutch courage never hurt anyone.

Actually, two whiskeys and diet Cokes never hurt anyone.

Before I know it, it's gone eight o'clock and I'm walking towards the party. Armed with Elle's gift and a smile painted on my face, I'm ready for the night ahead. No matter what, I'm here to have a good time.

"Oh my god, Mia!" Elle squeals excitedly as she pulls me in for a hug as soon as I walk through the front door. "You look so good! I love the dress!"

I'm so pleased Elle loves my look although she did gawp for a split second – perhaps it is a little revealing, but I guess it's too late now. Elle has gone for a floor-length gold sequin backless dress and her beautiful red hair is all brushed over and clipped back to one side with tight curls, very classy.

"Thank you so much, the place looks amazing," I say sincerely as I admire the flamboyant roaring twenties decor.

"I had specialist party designers in! Isn't it fab?"

"It really is. You definitely know how to throw a party. Happy birthday! Here's your gift, I wasn't sure what to get you, but I hope you like it."

"Thank you darling, you didn't have to! I'll put it on the table and then I want you to come and meet my friends," she says forcefully as she takes me by the hand and leads me towards the kitchen.

I notice she's sipping on champagne and seems a little tipsy already, although maybe I just pick up on these things more now that I know she has an issue with drinking.

The house really does look incredible – I feel like I have stepped back in time and everyone around me seems to have made a huge effort. There must be at least two hundred people here. There's even a live band – the music is loud, the drinks are flowing, it really is in full swing and the atmosphere is buzzing.

"Darling, this is my friend Lizzie, we've known each other since school, and this is Beatrice, she's married to one of Daddy's friends, they're golfing buddies and that's how we met. Ladies, this is my neighbour Mia."

"Pleasure, Mia," Lizzie nods with a small smile and I offer a polite smile back.

"Where's your husband?" Beatrice asks.

"Mia is divorced, remember ladies? I told you already." Elle snorts as if it's ground-breaking news that they shouldn't have forgotten.

"Sorry to hear that," Beatrice follows up with.

"It's fine honestly, I'm a lot happier now. I'm just concentrating on my career at the moment."

"Oh? And what do you do?" Lizzie enquires.

"I'm a sports journalist, I have my own columns."

"Sports?!" Beatrice scoffs. "I didn't know women got jobs in sports!?"

Lizzie and Elle join in with her mocking as they giggle like schoolgirls behind their champagne flutes.

"Yes, and we also vote now too," I reply sarcastically. Jacob was right about this at least; they really aren't my sort of people.

"Oh Mia, you're such a hoot!" Elle laughs theatrically, as if I just made a brilliant joke. It instantly plays down my comment, although I wish it didn't.

I smile politely but all I know is that I want to get away from Lizzie and Beatrice as quickly as possible. I'm not nearly drunk enough for this.

"I hope you don't mind if I excuse myself, I'm just going to get a drink."

"Of course, darling, then come and find me again because I have a surprise for you," Elle calls after me as I make my way to the makeshift bar.

I dread to think what the surprise could be. Hopefully not another stuck-up, narrow-minded friend though.

I order myself a gin and tonic and stay at the bar for a few extra moments before going to find Elle.

As I take a sip of my drink, I feel as though someone is watching me. To my surprise, I see Jacob sitting at a table in the corner with a couple of other guys around his age. I really like what he is wearing, a crisp white shirt with black braces and a matching tie. It's kind of quirky but definitely in keeping with the theme. I notice his eyes studying me, gazing down to my legs and back up to my waist, chest and face, before they wander back down again. My skin feels like it's on fire just knowing he is examining my body so carefully.

I turn my back and sashay away to find Elle. I wouldn't want to stand there for too long and have him thinking I'm crushing on him again. I wouldn't want his stupid ego growing any more than it has.

"This is who I was telling you about, this is Mia," Elle says as she approaches me with a silver-haired man on her arm.

He grins instantly, showing his very white American smile. He then stares straight to my chest and makes no secret of it either.

"Erm, hi?" I greet him a little bemused.

"Wow, you're gorgeous. Elle said you were, but wow."

"Mia, this is Patrick. He is also a lawyer but works for a different firm now. He is single too," Elle says, practically pushing Patrick onto me.

I'm unimpressed to say the least. Patrick is handsome I guess, but a lot older than me, he must be late forties I would have thought, and he already comes across as quite sleazy.

"Nice to meet you," I say politely, although I'm contemplating whipping these heels off and running for the front door. There is nothing that makes me cringe more than someone trying to set me up.

"Why don't I let you two get acquainted?"

"Sure Elle, thank you. I can take over from here," Patrick answers for us as he studies my lips.

All I can think of is how I wish I had a flare gun. I might not be at sea but surely this warrants a distress signal.

Chapter twelve

"You certainly have dressed to catch a few eyes, haven't you?" Patrick jeers at me, while staring at my chest again.

"Well, just trying to mimic a woman from the twenties," I answer quietly. I came here for a good night and this really wasn't what I had in mind. I feel so uncomfortable, I have nothing to talk to this man about and it's obvious he only really wants one thing and I'm not the one to give it to him.

"So, Mia, tell me about yourself?"

"Uh, well I'm a sports journalist, I moved here only recently from London and that's about it really, I don't have anything that interesting going on at the moment." I giggle awkwardly. "How about you?"

"Well, I'm a lawyer. In the last five years I have taken over three law firms and last year I made my first million. Does that interest you?" he says with a flirtatious smirk as if all women gush at the mention of his wealth.

"Err...well, congratulations. I'm sure you worked very hard for it."

"A double gin and tonic for the lady, please," Patrick says to the hired bartender. Oh brilliant, now he's trying to get me drunk. What a classy move. Dickhead.

"Double? I was just drinking singles."

"Oh, come on Mia. Don't be so boring." Patrick winks at me

suggestively.

"Erm, okay, just the one double then." I try to force a smile but inside I feel ready to go home. I have only been here an hour but so far, I haven't had any fun.

"I'm just going to nip upstairs to the bathroom first, I won't be long."

"Ok, baby. See you in a minute. I'll look after your drink."

Eurgh. Baby. Cringe.

I make my way upstairs to Elle's bathroom and splash some water on my chest and neck. I don't know why but I have suddenly come over with anxiety. I haven't suffered with it in so long but tonight I feel so uncomfortable. I just don't seem to fit in here and to top it off, it looks like my night is going to be spent standing with a creep whose only interest in me is what's underneath my dress.

Deep breaths Mia, I tell myself over and over. Stay calm.

I can excuse myself and go home, I don't have to stay. I have been polite, I came by for Elle, I dropped her off a birthday present and now I'm sure it's fine if I leave. I take a deep breath and readjust my dress in the mirror and spruce up my hair a little bit. One more drink and then I'll go.

As I open the bathroom door, I'm surprised to see Jacob leaning against the wall with his arms folded and his typically stern look on his face.

"Mia?" He looks at me sheepishly.

"Yes?"

"Why are you talking to Patrick?"

"I don't know really...Elle introduced us and now he's just getting me a drink."

"He's no good for you Mia. I wasn't going to get involved but I saw the way he was gawping at you..."

"Gawping at me?" I question with almost a giggle. "And why does that worry you?"

"It doesn't. But you're too good for him. Trust me when I tell you he isn't good news."

I can't help but roll my eyes at his unpredictable attitude towards me. I can't be bothered to entertain him a minute longer; he keeps doing this, and then any second now he'll be back to insulting me again. I flick my hair back out of my face and attempt to walk past him, but he grabs me by the arm.

"I'm serious Mia, he doesn't treat women well. Make your excuses and go home."

"Why should I listen to you?"

"For god's sake Mia. I'm trying to help you here. Just for once, just trust what I'm saying and do as I ask you."

"Jeez...okay, okay! I'm going to finish my drink and then I'll go home, now get off me will you." I pull my arm away irritably and dart down the stairs before he has a chance to stop me again.

This guy is so up and down he confuses me so much. Usually, I wouldn't take a blind bit of notice, but I think he has a point with Patrick. I haven't exactly gotten the best feeling from him.

"There she is! I was beginning to think you'd gotten lost," Patrick says, laughing at his own terrible joke and passing me my gin.

"Thank you so much. That's really kind of you, but to be honest I have a little bit of a headache so I think I might head home after this one."

"That's a shame…" he says as he leans over to whisper in my ear. "Because I really thought we were about to have some fun."

I wince as I feel his hand slide over the small of my back and then travel down until he tightly grasps my cheek in his palm.

"I'm sure there are lots of people here who would love your company," I suggest awkwardly.

I take a step back and sit on a bar stool, so he has no choice but to remove his hand from behind me. Suddenly, I'm a lot thirstier – if I can quickly finish this gin with a few large gulps then I can get out of here.

"None of them are in a tight dress though, are they?"

"Here's your drinks, sir," the bartender interrupts as he passes me another double gin and tonic.

"What?" I ask.

Patrick grins. "I got another round in when you were in the bathroom. I can't turn it away now, can I?"

"I suppose not."

Quickly, I tilt my head back and knock down the last gulp of the gin, before reluctantly picking up the next. I'll drink this one as quickly as I can too and then I'll be out of here.

I'm really starting to wish I'd eaten some dinner earlier because my stomach is so empty; I didn't expect I would be drinking this much so quickly. My head is definitely beginning to feel quite light.

"So, Elle said you live opposite? The house with all the glass?"

"Yep. That's right," I confirm, although I really wish Elle hadn't told him that.

"Wow, I bet it's a nightmare to clean those."

"Yeah...I hadn't really thought about it, but I suppose it would be."

"Well it's good news then that I happen to know a fantastic window cleaner isn't it? I have his business card in my car, I'll give it to you before you leave."

"Great. That's really helpful," I say before using this as an opportunity to gulp down the rest of my drink and make my way home. "Well, I'm ready now?"

"Oh right, okay, well my car is right out front."

I turn around quickly to see if I can spot Elle through the crowd of people, but I can't seem to find her at all. She could be in the garden but it's even busier out there. I'm sure she won't mind if I just sneak off, she's busy anyway with all her other friends. I can always thank her for the invite tomorrow.

I head to the front door with Patrick following closely behind. The fresh air hits me as soon as I step outside; I'm definitely feeling the effects of having to drink my gin so fast. I can hear my stomach growling too. I'm looking forward to making a cup of tea and a couple of slices of buttery toast as soon as I get indoors.

"My car is over here," Patrick says as he gestures to the black jeep tucked in the corner of the driveway. "Come over and I'll see if I can fish that card out for you."

I nod reluctantly and try to seem grateful for a business card that I don't particularly want, but I know the quicker I humour him and take the card, the quicker I can get home.

I hover awkwardly whilst Patrick rummages around in his car. Although it's nearly summer, it's cold tonight; my teeth are chattering, and my body is shivering whilst I wait.

"I can't seem to find it," Patrick eventually informs me.

"Oh, it's fine, really. I'm sure I'll find one online but thank you anyway."

"Well look, why don't I take you out for dinner next week? I might have found the card by then."

"I... well, it's okay. Really. I'm so busy lately and I just got through a messy divorce, I'm not really looking for a relationship."

"Who said anything about a relationship?" Patrick grins as he takes a step towards me. Behind him I can just about make out Jacob; he's still upstairs, only now he's standing at his office window, watching.

"Okay then Mia, what about just a goodnight kiss?"

"I can't, I'm sorry," I stutter awkwardly. "Goodnight."

But as I turn to walk away, Patrick steps in front of me and pushes me hard against his car. With his foot he kicks my legs apart and tries pulling up my skirt.

"Come on baby, just a little bit of fun," he whispers as his tongue slides across my neck.

"Stop, Patrick. Stop!" I yell. I try to push him off, but he is stronger than me and I'm in so much shock I feel as though my legs are numb. I want to run away, but I can't move. I feel paralysed against the cold hard door.

"Baby, if you can't handle the attention then don't wear a fucking dress like that," he says as he slams me again against his car in frustration.

Before I have a chance to react, Patrick is on the floor. His body is no longer pressing me against his car.

How?

I look down to see Jacob towering over Patrick. With one hand he has a hold of Patrick's collar and with the other he makes a fist and hits him hard. And then does it again. And again. It's all happening so fast, but Jacob won't stop punching him. Blood is pouring from Patrick's face. It's becoming like a scene from a horror movie.

"Jesus…Jacob, enough! Stop!" I bellow, but he doesn't respond. I watch on, terrified of what Jacob could do to him as he continues to rain punches down onto him.

"JACOB!" I hear a man shout as he comes running from the front of the house with two of the guys, I saw Jacob sitting with earlier. They're quick to rush over and pull him off Patrick, but they're seconds too late. There is barely a spot left on Patrick's face that isn't covered in blood and he looks barely conscious.

My heart is thumping against my chest and my head is fuzzy; I feel as though I could pass out.

"What the hell happened?" one of his friends asks as he pulls Jacob to his feet.

"You could have killed him," another says.

"The party is over. Get everyone out of my fucking house," Jacob says, out of breath, before giving me a sorrowful look and walking back into the house.

Chapter thirteen

I'm shaking so much I can barely hold the vodka still long enough to pour it into my glass. I never drink vodka straight but if there ever was a time to try it, it's now.

Despite feeling tipsy earlier, I'm certainly sober as a judge now. The shock of what just happened made sure of that. I don't even think it was Patrick's actions that shocked me the most, but rather Jacob who has left me speechless. Jacob is well-built, I know that, I've seen his body, and the fact he has his own gym at home shows me how into fitness he is, so I know he is strong and capable if he has to defend himself. But I had no clue he could or would ever fight like that.

I down my vodka with one swig as I watch all the party guests scramble out of Jacob's house. One of Jacob's friends seems to be pulling Patrick up onto his feet and carrying him to a car, I'm assuming they're taking him home. Elle is standing by the front door looking as though she is about to cry and throw an almighty tantrum. It's obvious she's angry and has no real clue as to what's just gone on.

My nerves are calming a little bit and I notice my body has stopped trembling; the vodka has done what I hoped and settled my anxiety. I grab my sofa blanket and wrap it round my shoulders to help me warm up too. I'm not sure what to do with myself; my adrenaline is still pumping enough that I know I won't be able to sleep, and my mind is racing with thoughts of Jacob and wondering whether he is okay.

Thanks to Patrick, I really don't like this dress anymore. I just had a flashback of him aggressively trying to pull up my skirt and I don't think I'll ever want to wear it again. In fact, I want to bin it right now. I zip myself out of it and toss it straight into the kitchen bin and then I head upstairs to find a basic white tee and some jeans to wear instead.

I sit at my make-up table and carefully wipe away the mascara from my eyes and the smudged red lipstick from where Patrick was trying to kiss me. I think back to Jacob warning me off outside the bathroom. Oh, how I wish now that I had just come straight home.

When I glance back out of my window and towards the house, I see that everyone has now left and it's a lot quieter. The music from the live band is no longer playing and the majority of the lights are off; you wouldn't even know there had been a party if it wasn't for the few plastic cups scattered around the driveway.

This could be my opportunity to go back over, I could offer Elle a helping hand in tidying everything up, but I could also try to get a moment alone with Jacob to thank him for helping me.

I throw my white trainers on and head downstairs before I can talk myself out of it.

I half expect to hear arguing as I get closer to the house, but nothing. I lightly knock on the door just in case they've gone to bed.

"Mia?" Elle croaks as she pulls open the door. Her eyes are puffy, and she has mascara streaks down her face; she's clearly been crying.

"Hey," I say sympathetically. "I thought I could maybe help you tidy up?"

"That's sweet but I don't expect you to. I'm sorry the party was ruined. Did you have fun before my husband decided to kick everyone out?"

"I had an amazing time," I lie. "Please don't apologise. You have nothing to be sorry for."

Elle gestures me in and I follow behind her as she leads the way to the lounge, an area of the house I haven't spent much time in before.

"He ruined everything," Elle whines dramatically as she slumps down into an armchair. "All I know is that he was seen fighting with someone on the driveway. But he won't tell me who it was or why."

"Perhaps it was just a silly alcohol-fuelled fight. You know what men can be like."

"Not Jacob," Elle says defensively. "We don't engage in fights. Jacob knows full well how I feel about violence. He has completely shown me up tonight in front of all our guests and he hasn't even got the good grace to tell me why."

I fidget awkwardly by the lounge door, I'm not really sure what I can do or say right now. I know why Jacob got into a fight but if he doesn't want to tell Elle why it happened, then I really shouldn't either.

"I'm going to bed. I have a huge migraine and due to the stress, I've been forced to take a sleeping tablet. If you really want to help with the mess, Jacob is outside picking up rubbish, I'm sure he could use a hand."

I nod politely to show I'm happy to help and watch as Elle disappears off upstairs. When I hear her close her bedroom door behind her, I take a deep breath and head off through to the kitchen and out into the garden to find Jacob.

I spot him immediately – he isn't actually tidying up, but is sitting by the pool, feet dangling in and a bag of ice on his hand.

"Jacob?" I say so quietly it almost comes out as a whisper.

He looks up at me straightaway with a frown as if he can't understand why I would be here, but after a split second his frown fades and he look somewhat pleased to see me.

"Erm, Elle said I could come out and give you a hand with tidying up. She's gone to bed."

I approach with caution, unsure of which attitude from Jacob I'll get. I grab a seat on a sun lounger next to the pool.

"Jacob, listen. I am so sorry about tonight. When you warned me, I should have just left, I shouldn't have questioned you and..."

"Sorry?" Jacob cuts me off. "You have nothing to be sorry for. Why would you think you do?"

"I ruined your party. I made you get into a fight," I answer apologetically.

"You didn't make me do anything Mia." Jacob grabs a small glass filled with a brown liquor from next to him and takes a large mouthful. "When I saw Pat... that scumbag, touch you the way he did, I felt sick. All I knew at that moment was that I had to protect you."

I smile to myself at his words. I feel butterflies in my stomach over how sweet he is being.

"Will it get you into trouble?"

"Fuck no," Jacob says with a chuckle. "If he tells anyone what I did then he'll have to explain why I did it and he won't want that."

Jacob throws back another mouthful of his liquor before staring at me with sorrow in his eyes.

"Are you okay, after…after what happened?"

"I think so," I try to reassure him. "Thanks to you, I'm okay."

"You know…I had just over two hundred guests tonight and I can barely tolerate any of them. They're not my people, this isn't the lifestyle I wanted. But then I saw you and I thought, finally, someone I can relate to. Let's just say I'm pleased you're stubborn and don't listen when someone tries to uninvite you to their party," he says with a big smile and I can't help but giggle.

"Will you stay and have a drink with me, Mia?"

"Sure," I answer without hesitation and feel the butterflies return to my stomach.

"Get comfortable and I'll get us both a drink."

I watch on contentedly; my eyes stay on Jacob whilst he heads back inside to fix us a drink. I feel like this is the most honest conversation we've had with each other so far, and it's only just beginning.

"Here," Jacob says as he puts a blanket around my shoulders. "Just in case you get cold."

I love his warmth and smile gratefully as he passes me a neat whiskey.

"Something has been on my mind for a little while and I feel as though I should explain it. The other day you accused me of sleeping with Elle's best friend?"

"Oh. Yeah, I did," I answer timidly. "I shouldn't have thrown your past at you. I'm sorry."

"No, I'm pleased you did, because it gives me a chance to clear a few things up. You're the one person who I don't want to think badly of me."

I sit back on the sun lounger so I'm comfortable and I show him that I'm listening. I'm nervous about the answer, but I'm listening.

"To explain everything honestly, I'll need to start from the very beginning. It could take some time."

I reach out and give his hand a little comforting squeeze.

"I'm not going anywhere, Jacob."

Chapter fourteen

It's quite cold outside now but the soft blanket around my shoulders keeps me warm enough. One thing I have enjoyed about moving out of the city is how many stars you can see at night. There are so many, each one so beautifully lit up, so wonderfully calming.

Jacob's lips are tightly pressed as he swirls the ice around his glass.

"I'm guessing you have heard of arranged marriages?" he eventually starts as he looks at me with worried eyes.

"Of course, but I'm not a particularly religious person, so I can't say I've witnessed any."

"They aren't always to do with religion. Sometimes it can be about the class you're in – for instance, some rich families strongly believe that if you come from wealth, you should marry someone who is equally wealthy or at the very least comes from a privileged background. Unfortunately, this was Elle's father's view, and my dad also felt it was a good idea, and since I was nineteen, he put a lot of pressure on me to get married."

"Oh, I see..."

"I was young, stressed to bits trying to get my law degree to appease my dad and then on top of all that, he kept arranging for Elle to come to the house. We had nothing in common and she quite openly told me she had no ambition to have a career, she felt her calling in life was to be a housewife. My dad and Elle's dad decided together that we were some kind of match made in heaven. My dad felt as though any woman I could meet wouldn't be right for me and would only want our family fortune. Ironically, the exact person he was so concerned about is the very woman he pushed me to marry."

"But I thought Elle had money?"

"She comes from wealth, but she doesn't have her own money. That's why her dad wanted her to be with me, he wanted me to look after her."

"Wow," I sigh, trying to take it all in.

"Elle doesn't love me. She might say she does, she's good at saying all the right things, but the only thing she truly loves is my bank account and this lifestyle. She needs a status to feel like she's something. It's sad really."

"Is that why she drinks?"

"I think so. Her dad ended up as an alcoholic too, so I'm guessing it's in the family. Neither of us have been happy for a long time. Then Elle's friend goes missing one night and she asks me to go out and find her. Usually I don't like to get involved in these things, but I felt sorry for her, her husband had just died, and she was a mess.

"I tracked her down in a pub near her house, she was drunk and not in a good way. I told her I was there to take her home and she seemed grateful at first, until we got in the car and she wanted much more from me. She climbed onto my lap and tried straddling me and kissing me."

I feel a pang of jealousy as I picture someone all over him. I didn't believe I was the jealous type, but I hate this image he has painted.

"I may not love my wife but that doesn't mean I want to go sleeping with just anyone. She's not my type and I knew she wouldn't want to betray Elle, so I pushed her off. I made it clear that I had absolutely no interest. That's when she got angry. I thought she was just acting out because she was drunk. I dropped her home and thought no more about it, but the next day she turned up at the house and started telling Elle that I fucked her. I think it was my punishment for not taking her up on her offer."

He pauses to refill our glasses with the whiskey, and I find myself growing sympathetic as I hear the emotion grow in his voice and see the glimmer of sadness in his eyes.

"And that's when I knew for certain that Elle didn't love me. When her friend told her, she didn't cry. She didn't yell. She didn't throw things at me, she didn't scream at me to pack my bags and leave, she didn't even ask me if it was true. I realised then that she didn't ask me because she didn't actually care. I gave her space for a few days, I waited to see if she was just gathering her thoughts, but nothing.

"That's when I approached her and proposed a divorce. She hated the idea. She told me straightaway that it wasn't an option. She told me she didn't care about what I had supposedly gotten up to, as long as our lifestyle together could remain the same."

Shit. That's worse than any answer I could have imagined.

"I'm so sorry Jacob. I got out of my unhappy marriage; I can't imagine how it must feel to be stuck in one."

"Yeah well...life isn't always what we dreamt it could be." He sighs before taking another sip of his whiskey.

"Funny isn't it, people assume that because we have a big house and a tonne of photos on display that we must love our life together and be very happy. Reality is, it couldn't be further from the truth. But together we put on a good show."

I'm sitting here staring up at the stars, trying to think of anything to say that could be of comfort. But I truly feel lost for words. He's trapped. His marriage is about money, status and keeping up appearances. Elle doesn't even care what he does, as long as she has this house and the big cars and holidays to Aruba. Meanwhile, Jacob looks like a broken man. No wonder he can be so angry.

"How's your hand?" I ask gently as I stare down at the grazes across his knuckles.

"Better."

"Good. You think it'll be okay to get in the hot tub?"

"Really? You want to get into the hot tub now? It's nearly two in the morning!" Jacob laughs.

"I know. And we're the only ones awake."

I put my glass down and slowly unzip my jeans. I let them drop to my feet as Jacob stares at me intensely and I step out of them before heading to the hot tub.

I carefully dip my toe into the hot water before immersing myself fully. I can't help but smile when I see Jacob heading over too, pulling his shirt off over his head.

I giggle to myself as Jacob notices my breasts through my white tee. I hadn't bothered with a bra and now I'm glad I didn't. The water has made my top see through and I love how much it excites him.

"Mia, what are we doing?" Jacob asks through heavy breaths as he lowers himself into the hot tub.

"Don't worry. I'm not expecting you to do anything."

I gently push against his shoulders until he is seated in front of me.

"But...I think I started something I didn't get to finish the other night."

I slide my knickers down my legs and let them float to the surface. The surprise on Jacob's face makes me giggle.

I pull my white tee over my head and throw it to the side, leaving my breasts free to bob gently against the water.

"Shit, Mia," Jacob pants excitedly.

I perch on the edge of the step and keep my eyes focused on Jacob.

"Tell me you want to watch me. I want to hear you say it."

"Fuck, Mia. Yes. Yes, I want to fucking watch."

I seductively arch my back before running my fingers down my stomach, past my hip bone until eventually I'm sliding them inside of me.

My skin feels so tingly just knowing Jacob is watching me. It's such a buzz and I know it won't take me long.

I love the undeniable flash of arousal in his eyes, it makes me want to excite him further. With one hand I grip my breast tightly before running my fingers in a circular motion and caressing my nipples.

I feel the heat rushing in between my legs and I let out a few quiet groans to let Jacob know I'm close.

"Fuck..." I hear Jacob groan as he watches my fingers sliding in and out of myself.

I can't believe I'm back doing this again but it's so different, it's so spontaneous, so unpredictable and I love it. I love knowing I have Jacob in the palm of my hand. I love knowing I'm exciting him just as much as he excites me.

"Finish for me Mia," Jacob pants just as an erotic shock jolts through my body and I bite down hard on my lip as I reach climax. The dizzying mix of my intense orgasm and the adrenaline of getting caught leaves me exhausted.

When I eventually get my breath back, I pull my head forward and lock eyes with Jacob who may as well have his jaw on the floor. I laugh at his expression, before carefully leaving the hot tub.

"I thought I'd leave you with something to tide you over for a while," I say with a domineering look. "Goodnight, Jacob."

Chapter fifteen

The tiredness after only a few hours' sleep has kicked in, but I smile to myself when I recall how worth it was.

I knew there was something wrong between Jacob and Elle, but I had no idea it was quite so broken. I thought maybe they were just going through a marital blip, maybe Elle spends too much money or Jacob spends too much time with his friends, you know, the kind of things couples can argue about. I didn't for a moment suspect that they were in some kind of money-driven arranged marriage.

I can't imagine the stress Jacob has felt trying to please his father. That's something I never had to worry about. My dad was a supermarket manager by trade, so money and status were never a factor in my upbringing. In fact, Dad used to tell me that he didn't care what I did in life, just as long as I was happy. So, I used to joke and say that I'd come to work every day with him, and he'd just laugh and tell me that as long as I woke up every day happy to go to work, then I could. My dad was so laid back and understanding. He was proud when I went to university, but I know he would have been just as proud if I had chosen to clean toilets for a living.

Listening to Jacob last night, I know now that his upbringing wasn't as relaxed as mine. I love that we connected as much as we did though, I love that he shared so much about himself with me.

I'm driving to Bedfordshire today for a wedding; my cousin Sara is finally getting married to her childhood sweetheart. She pushed me to invite a plus one but seeing as Jacob isn't an option then I'm happy to go on my own. Although he is all I can think about today.

I hope he isn't getting too much of an earache from Elle today for ruining her party. I hate that she's more concerned over what her guests think than about her husband's bloodied knuckles and trying to support him and make sure he is okay. She said it herself that it was out of character, but rather than try to understand why, she arrogantly only wants to hear an explanation and an apology.

As I pull up to the breathtaking Manor House, I see a crowd of people waiting to be seated; most of them are standing together as couples. I'm really starting to wish I had brought a plus one now – even Puss would have done.

Sara certainly picked a beautiful day to get married, the skies are blue, with barely a cloud to be seen and the sun is shining down brightly. The grounds really are amazing. I shouldn't be thinking it, but I bet this cost a pretty penny.

A few people notice I'm alone as I walk up to the entrance to be seated and give me a friendly nod and a smile. I know it's their way of being polite, but it really makes me feel like a bit of a loser. I decide to take a seat near the back on my own.

Sara looks stunningly elegant when she appears at the doorway. Her deep chocolate brown hair is pinned up beautifully in a kind of 1930's style, which doesn't surprise me, Sara loves anything old fashioned and vintage. Her dress is mostly lace and sits perfectly just off the shoulders. It's a really classy dress and I actually feel quite emotional watching her exchange her vows on the happiest day of her life.

I spent quite a lot of time with Sara and Auntie May when I was growing up. I had to since Mum was always on the cruise ships and Dad was working over forty hours a week in the supermarket. I have a lot of fond memories of us running around the garden naked in the summer and splashing around in a tiny paddling pool. Giggling and pretending we were mermaids. Sounds a bit weird now the more I think about it, but that was the eighties for you.

I'm dreading finding out where I'm sitting in the reception room. My mind casts back to an old *Friends* episode where Ross had to sit next to the kids at Monica and Chandler's wedding. God, I have a feeling that'll be me today. Thankfully it's not quite that bad, I'm sitting on what can only be described as the pensioners' table, but at least I'm seated next to my grandmother; it'll be nice to have a catch up with her.

At least I thought so, until I remembered about her hearing difficulties and memory loss.

"Where's Alex?" Gran asks loudly with a confused expression on her face.

"He isn't here Gran, we got divorced, remember?"

"Who did?"

"Alex and I, we got divorced," I'm forced to announce again and louder this time.

"No. That didn't happen. I came to your wedding."

"I know Gran, we were married but now we are divorced."

"Is Alex at work?"

"Yes, he's training hard and couldn't make it," I lie. I'm sure as hell not repeating that again and again.

It would make a good drinking game though; I could take a shot every time she asks me where Alex is. I'd be pissed before the starters even make it out.

I'm already taking full advantage of the basket full of crusty bread rolls on our table; they're still hot from the oven and the fresh smell is too delicious to ignore.

"Save some room for your dinner, Mia."

"Yes, Gran," I answer, trying to hold back my giggle at her fussing over me. Even at my age.

Just as I'm about to reach for my second roll, I see Sara waving to get my attention by the ladies' toilets. *Come here!* I see her mouth to me.

"I'll be back in a second Gran; I just need to pop to the ladies," I say as I excuse myself and head over to a flustered-looking Sara.

As soon as I approach her, she practically pulls me into the toilets by my arm, frantically.

"Quick, hide with me for a minute or two," she puffs, out of breath.

"What's going on?"

"I just want one minute without someone asking me when I'm going to start having babies! Honestly, it's like now I'm married, the natural progression is to pop out sprogs! I'm not ready for that!"

"Ah yeah, I had that a lot at my wedding too. People just get ahead of themselves."

"Here… drink this with me," she says as she pulls out two miniature bottles of tequila from her bra.

"Classy broad!" I say with sarcasm. "But I've got to drive home, I can't really drink."

"Oh, one won't hurt. Come on Mia, be wild."

I reluctantly agree and take the bottle from her as a big smirk lights up her face. How can I say no on her wedding day?

"Speaking of being wild. What have you gotten up to since Alex? Are you seeing anyone?"

"I'm still single," I say as she pulls a pretend mocking yawn.

"Mia! Come on, you're young. You're newly divorced, this is a chance to finally let your hair down, go and sow some wild oats! You play everything so safe, honestly. You won't find fun just sitting at home working and talking to yourself."

"Oh really?" I smirk back with one eyebrow arched. "You want to hear something wild?"

She nods excitedly.

"Okay, last night I went over to my neighbour's house, got naked in his hot tub and forced him to watch me pleasure myself all whilst his Mrs was asleep upstairs. Is that wild enough for you?"

"Pah! Yeah right!" she explodes through cackled laughter.

I keep my eyes on her until she realises, I'm being deadly serious.

"Oh fuck! You're not kidding?"

"Nope. I'm being serious."

"Holy fuck! So, what is this then? Are you having an affair?"

The question takes me by surprise.

"Well...I don't know. I don't think so. I mean, I did that, but he hasn't actually touched me. We haven't even kissed."

"But you did that in his hot tub...Jesus, Mia. When I said crazy, I meant like having a one-night stand with a single guy you met through a dating app, I didn't mean getting naked in a married man's hot tub," she says with an element of judgement in her tone.

"It's not like that...we have a bit of a spark. They're both in an unhappy marriage."

"That's what they all say!"

"No, really. They had an arranged marriage; they were never even in love. They were just put together for convenience."

"Okay...so, when is he going to leave his wife?"

"Well he hasn't said. We haven't discussed that. I don't think..."

"Mia! He won't leave his wife! Come on, you're a bit of skirt across the street. He'll have his cake and eat it," Sara interrupts.

"Sara..." I groan impatiently. She doesn't understand at all.

"Mia, I'm only saying it because I don't want you to get hurt. If things are that bad with his wife and you two have such a spark, then why isn't he chasing you?"

"Well, it's complicated. His wife, Elle, she's having issues."

I can tell by Sara's unimpressed expression that nothing I am saying is changing how she feels about the idea. She doesn't know the full extent of Elle; she doesn't know Jacob. She can't possibly know what I mean to him.

"Do me a favour. Think about it for a few days, ask yourself if he is worth the shit-tonne of grief this is going to cause. Is he actually committed to you? Or is he just excited by the thought of you?"

I nod to keep her happy and take the last mouthful of the miniature tequila. I almost wish I hadn't told her now. I feel like she just burst any bubble I had.

"Right, I got to get back out there before my new husband wonders where I am! Love ya!" she says and plants a kiss on my cheek before picking up her wedding dress from the floor and walking out of the bathroom, leaving me behind to ponder on our conversation.

Chapter sixteen

"Where's Alex?" Gran asks again when I finally return to my seat.

Why did Sara have to put all that doubt in my mind? An hour ago, I couldn't stop smiling and now I'm worried and doubting the way Jacob feels about me.

"Is Alex parking the car?"

I mean, it's one thing if we had met and fallen in love, but a whole different story if we are just having some seedy affair. I know what I have done so far is hardly romantic, it's definitely seedier, but that's because I thought we were having fun to start with. I wanted to create some excitement.

"I can't wait to have a catch up with Alex, is he coming now Mia? He can sit next to me if he likes."

I don't know how I feel about potentially being the *other* woman. I don't expect Jacob to go packing his bags right this second. But maybe at some point he should be planning that, right?

"Mia? Where's your husband?"

"He's not my fucking husband, Gran!" I snap and regret it instantly. Oh god, I just shouted at my eighty-seven-year-old Gran. Please can the ground swallow me now.

I look up to see my Gran's shocked face as she stares timidly in my direction. Unsure of what to do next, she takes a sip of her sherry and doesn't ask me another thing. I feel like the smallest person in the world.

"Gran...Gran, listen to me. I am not with Alex anymore. I'm sorry if that upsets you," I say as clearly and as loudly as I can.

"Why would that upset me?"

"Because...because I know you loved him."

"Well, yes. But not as much as I love you," she responds. Making me feel even more like the biggest twat on the planet.

I feel tears stinging my eyes at her soft kind words. Never in my entire life have I raised my voice at my Gran, and I am so ashamed of myself to have done it now. I swallow hard and try to get rid of the horrible lump that's gathered in my throat. I don't want to be here anymore. All I can think of is diving into my bed and being alone.

"Gran...I'm so sorry. I haven't been myself," I say, and she nods as if she understands. I wouldn't expect anything less. She is so kind and I'm just a huge knobhead.

"I'm going to go home. I'm not feeling well. I love you, Gran."

I lean over and give her a kiss on the cheek. She embraces me with a cuddle, and I have to work even harder to hide my emotions. I ponder for a second about whether I should say goodbye to Sara first, after all, it's the polite thing to do but I can see her smiling brightly on the dance floor with her arms draped around her new husband and I just can't bring myself to walk over there.

My chest feels heavy with sadness and I just want to curl up in bed with a good book or shove my headphones in and fall asleep listening to good music. I dodge most distant family members to save myself from the excruciating pain of small talk. Thankfully, I'm out of there fairly unnoticed and I make a beeline for my Lexus. Once in the safety of my car I can finally let out a big sigh. Like the relief when you take a tight corset off, I feel like I can breathe.

I'm grateful that the traffic is light, and I make it home in around an hour and a half. Not too bad. As I pull into our cul-de-sac, I notice most of the lights are on in Jacob's house. I picture him and Elle drinking wine and laughing together. I don't know why because I know that that's not how they are together. But suddenly I'm doubting everything since Sara's polite warning. The bottom line is, they live together, and they're still married, and I don't know how long for. What if it's years until Jacob leaves her? Would I wait for him? Would I actually put my own life on hold? I shudder at the thought. I couldn't do that to myself, I wouldn't.

Oh god. Oh god. Oh god. It's Elle. She's sitting on my doorstep, head resting on her palm looking either pissed off or very bored. Shit, what if she knows already? Would Jacob have told her without warning me? I'm not sure he would have but maybe it just came out? Maybe they were arguing, and he just happened to let slip that we've been messing around?

I park the car and try to act as casual as possible.

"Mia! Finally! I thought I was going to be sat here all night! Shit...you look incredible darling!" she slurs, and I spot the red wine in her other hand.

Ah, she's wasted. I can't deal with a drunk Elle right now. I just want my bed.

"I brought a bottle over. Shall we have a drink and a catch up? I'm still raging over Jacob breaking up MY party..."

"Actually Elle..." I impatiently interrupt. "I have a huge migraine. I'm sorry, but I think it's best if I just sleep this one off."

"Oh," she squeaks, taken aback. "Um...what should I do?"

"I don't know. Go home and have an early night?"

I hate the fact that she looks so disappointed and uncertain of what to do with herself. I hate that she feels so lost. Great. More guilt.

"Okay. I'll see you another time then."

"Elle...wait..." I call after her. "Why don't you come over tomorrow around seven? I'll cook dinner and we can talk then."

"Yes! That'll be lovely." She smiles and her disappointment fades away. But my guilt doesn't.

It's awkward as hell being her friend now. At first, I felt in control and as if I knew what I was doing but now I'm not so sure of anything.

"Night Elle," I mumble before putting my key in the lock and hiding away in my home.

I go to the kitchen straightaway and start making myself a cup of hot chocolate. I don't really know why. It's not something I drink very often but I feel like I need comforting and I remember how Dad used to make this for me when I was little. If I ever fell off my bike and scraped my knee or something similar, he'd tell me he would make me a special hot chocolate with whipped cream and marshmallows and promise me it was magic, and it would make me feel better. It always did too.

As if she knew, I see Puss at the door scratching to come in. Somehow this little cat always seems to appear when I'm having a particularly bad day. I let her in without hesitation and lock the door behind us as she races up behind me and into my bedroom.

She has no reservations about jumping on my bed and getting herself comfortable. I love how confident and friendly she is, it really makes me smile.

100

I can't even be bothered tonight to take off my make-up or brush out my hair. Instead, I literally strip down to my underwear, leave my clothes scattered on the floor and climb into bed.

Puss instantly creeps up the bed closer to me and snuggles her head against my chin. Her purring is so loud, it's actually quite therapeutic. I feel a tear fall from the corner of my eye and drop onto my pillow. I feel like the world's shittiest person and I'm not sure what to do next. My heart and my head are in conflict and I feel at such a loss.

I lie and stare at the ceiling as thoughts invade my mind, mostly negative thoughts that just make me feel worse. Gran's face pops into my thoughts and I feel so guilty it's almost unbearable. My chin wobbles and I feel more tears watering my eyes. Everything is just so messed up now. It's so crazy how I married Alex, spent years with him and yet I have felt more excitement in the short time I have known Jacob. Makes me wonder how many people in the world are married but unhappy. Maybe they don't know they're unhappy, especially if they have nothing to compare it to. But now I've met Jacob, I realise I'm feeling things I had never felt before.

"Night, Puss," I whisper before turning my lamp out and pulling my duvet up high to hide my face. I don't think it'll be easy to fall asleep with all these worries rushing around my mind, but I have to try.

Chapter seventeen

"Muuum!" I shout a bit too abruptly into my phone.

"What?! Mia? Is that you?"

"Mum, thank god you answered. I really need to…"

"God, Mia has someone died?"

"No, nothing like that, but…"

"Mia! It's four o'clock in the morning here…" she groans restlessly.

"Oh. Sorry it's nine a.m. here. Where are you?"

"Fort Lauderdale. Is this important? I'm ever so tired…"

"Mum. I really need to talk to you. Something has been weighing so heavily on my mind and I really don't know who else I can talk to. I barely slept last night. Can you please talk, just for five minutes?"

"Ohhh," she yawns. "Okay, what's up?"

"Mum…what do you think about affairs? Like infidelity? Is there ever an exception where it's okay?"

"What are you talking about, Mia?"

"I just mean, I don't know really…" I stutter, trying to find the right words to explain myself. "Can an affair ever be forgiven? How do you know if it could be love? Real true love? In which case it would be worth it? Wouldn't it?"

My words are so jumbled; I know I'm not making any sense but how on earth do I ask the questions to get the advice I need without telling Mum that I've gotten caught up with a married man?

"Oh god…" Mum mumbles and somehow, I know she's now sitting up in bed. "Is this about me and your dad?"

"Huh? What? Why would it be about Dad?"

"You mentioned the affair…" Mum whispers nervously.

"I was talking about…wait, what are YOU talking about, Mum?" I ask alarmed, as realisation sets in.

Surely not.

Mum is quiet. I know she's gathering her thoughts, careful of what to say next. I know this only too well because I do it too, I get that from her.

"Mum!?" I snap impatiently. "What affair were you talking about?"

"I had an affair once," Mum mumbles so timidly I barely hear it.

"You cheated on Dad?" I croak, as guilty tears instantly sting my eyes. I don't even know what I'm guilty of, I didn't do it to him, but I hate that she did. My dad was such a loving man, who would have done anything for her, and she clearly walked all over him. I always knew she did anyway, she always got her own way, she came in and out of our lives as she pleased, and Dad let her.

"Yes. I had an affair many years ago. But your dad and I, we worked through it. He forgave me."

"How could you have done that to him? He loved you! He fucking loved you, Mum!" I snap, so appalled that I'm physically having to hold myself back from hurling a bunch of insults at her. My heart is racing, adrenaline has my body trembling. I'm so mad. I don't think I have ever been this mad at her in my life.

"WHEN?"

"When what?"

"WHEN did this happen?"

"How does that make any difference?" Mum asks hesitantly.

"It just does. To me, it does. When?"

"Mia..."

"WHEN?"

"Before I fell pregnant with you."

Wha-what?

"What do you mean, before?" I gasp, so upset that I can feel my cheeks flushing red and my eyes puffing up as tears effortlessly fall from them.

"Come on Mia, please don't make me spell it out for you," she groans guiltily.

I swallow hard, trying to clear my throat from the strain of my upset.

"Well I'm afraid you *are* going to have to spell it out for me," I hiss.

"Your dad will always be your dad. He adored you. He wanted you. He loved you."

"But he isn't my dad?"

"No… Well, he might be. We don't know for sure. We never did any tests. He decided he didn't want to know. To him, you were his daughter and no DNA test was going to tell him different."

The thought of my dad's kind heart unconditionally loving and raising a child who might not be his own makes my heart sink. I would do anything to be able to drive to his house now and hug him so tight. I would thank him for being the incredibly admirable and selfless man that he is…and tell him I love him so much. And if it's possible, I might even love him more now.

"Who was the other guy?" I say through sobs.

"He…he was a holiday maker."

"What?" I jeer through laughter. "Great! So how long was the affair? Two weeks!?"

"No more than a week," Mum answers honestly and I can hear the embarrassment in her voice.

"Hurting my dad was worth it for one week with some random man on a holiday?"

"I know, Mia! Believe me, I know." Mum surprises me by yelling back. "Don't you think I haven't regretted it a million times already?"

"Where was the other guy from? Do I look like him? Or do I look more like Dad?"

"I don't know. I can barely remember him. I don't even know where he came from, I think he had a slight Irish accent, but I can't be sure. It was crazy, I'm not sure what came over me. All I know is that when I was with him, I felt so much excitement, I couldn't ignore it. It was new. Different. I loved your dad, I promise I did, but this guy brought out a different side to me that I never knew I had. I'm sorry, I'm so sorry. You were the last person I would ever want to hurt. But that's my truth."

Her romanticised memory of her feelings towards this stranger reminds me of how I have felt about Jacob and it makes me feel stupid. Am I just caught up in a stupid pointless affair that will leave nothing but disarray and broken hearts?

"Talk to me, Mia. Is there anything else you want to know? Whilst we are being honest?"

"I just want to be left alone for a little while Mum, okay?" I ask but hang up the phone before she has a chance to answer.

I can't bear to spend another moment on the phone. Not only do I feel disgusted by her right now, but I feel disgusted by myself and the more I talk to her the more she reminds me of that. I wish I could go back in time and tell my dad to leave her. She didn't deserve him, and we could have spent the rest of our lives happy, together. Or who knows, maybe he would have gone on to meet somebody who actually deserved him, and they could have been truly happy, and he would have been well looked after. He deserved to feel that type of love and commitment.

Another tear drops from my cheek as I ache for my dad. It's so unjust how he could love so wholeheartedly and never once in his life get the same back.

Am I a hypocrite? All I feel is pure anger towards my mum and pure hurt and heartache for my dad and yet I'm involved with Jacob. How am I any better? Who am I to judge when I'm just as...just as...low?

Without thinking, I open up my email app and send off a brief message to my boss, explaining that I'm not feeling too well, and I'll be taking a couple of days off from work.

I have a weird relationship with food. I'm the biggest comfort eater I know and all I can think about right now is heading down to the supermarket, stocking up on ice cream, chocolate, crisps and cakes and locking myself away in my pyjamas.

I know full well that self-wallowing and stuffing my face with carbohydrates isn't the right answer, but it's the only answer I have right now.

Chapter eighteen

I may have gone a little overboard in the supermarket. Eighty-seven pounds later and all I bought was alcohol, ice cream, cake and treats for Puss. I definitely looked as though I was having a mid-life crisis to the cashier.

My hair is now scraped up into a scruffy bun, I have my comfortable fluffy sliders on and some old leggings and a baggy t-shirt that I got at a Cher concert many years ago. I wonder how sexy Jacob would find me right now. He'd probably run a mile.

I picked up a new watermelon vodka from the shop which I hadn't seen before and after one mouthful from my glass, I can already tell this is going to be dangerous. It barely tastes alcoholic; I could drink a pitcher of it in one sitting and not realise I'm casually getting pissed.

I'm almost half an hour into my favourite girly flick, *Thelma and Louise*. God, I really wish I could jump into a Ford Thunderbird, throw on some shades and just keep driving through the desert with my best friend. Although at this rate, it would be Puss in the passenger seat. I laugh at the thought before digging my spoon into the pot of cookie dough ice cream and shovelling it into my mouth, a bit like Kevin in *Home Alone* when he made himself a giant bowl of various scoops of ice cream when his parents left him behind and went to Paris.

I love how sometimes you can get completely lost in a movie but hear a quote from a character and place it into your own life. Like when Louise warns Thelma that "you get what you settle for" and I can't help but think of Elle and Jacob, settling for each other and how that must feel. I'm not naïve enough to think they have never had happy times and made some good memories, but I wonder about the strain it could cause, settling for someone who doesn't make your heart race every time their lips brush against yours.

Then I start thinking about myself and how I have behaved since leaving Alex. Later on, in the film, Louise says to Thelma, "You've always been crazy; this is just the first chance you've had to express yourself" and of course my mind immediately flashes back to seducing Jacob from my bedroom window and then again in his hot tub. I blush at the memory. It's strange, I feel so morally torn. I liked that Mia, she was fun, wild, living in the moment and acting so vicariously. But I have no idea if that's truly me.

I can't think about this right now though, it just confuses me and after the bombshell Mum dropped on me this morning, I already have so much on my mind, my head has been spinning. I can't even bring myself to think of the possibility that my wonderful dad isn't actually my biological dad because it would break my heart. Which is probably why he didn't want a DNA test; he didn't want to know. Sometimes ignorance is bliss, I guess.

A sudden gentle knock at my door snaps me out of my depressive thoughts and immediately fills me with anxiety. Shit. Who could that be?

Bollocks. I totally forgot about Elle. Oh god, I really can't be bothered with Elle tonight either. I just want time alone. Maybe if I tell her I feel unwell and she sees the state of me, she won't want to come in anyway.

I start fake coughing as I head to the front door and swing it open.

Well, pull my tits and call me Brenda. It's not Elle.

"Jacob!" I blurt, shocked.

Shit. Shit. Shit. I look like a massive slob. Fuck.

"Hey!" he says smiling widely, showing off his perfectly white teeth. "You look…"

"Like a fucking slob?" I interrupt.

"No." He laughs gently. "I was going to say you look like you're having a quiet night in."

"Oh. Yeah, something like that."

"Well, can I come in?"

"Absolutely! Just wait one second," I insist whilst I gently close the door and rush back into the living room.

Bollocks. Jacob definitely won't want to see my white granny pants hanging on the radiator or my junk food spread all over the coffee table like a greedy slob. I quickly grab everything from the coffee table and hide it behind my sofa. I throw my knickers under the sofa cushion and make sure everything looks partially acceptable before opening the door again.

"Hey! Come in." I smile and attempt a nonchalant manner.

As soon as the door closes behind him, he makes a quick lunge towards me and places his hand gently around the back of my neck and pulls me close before pushing his lips against mine.

"You look so beautiful!" he pants through flustered breaths and kisses me again.

The kiss totally takes me by surprise, but I don't stop it. His tongue gently slides over mine and I feel his hot breath against my lips as he passionately continues to push his tongue inside my mouth.

I can't believe what I'm wearing. In all the times I imagined our first kiss I certainly wasn't wearing an ice cream-stained baggy t-shirt.

"Fuck, I've missed you," he whispers into my mouth before pushing me back and up against my wall.

My heart is racing as he slides his hand up my shirt and caresses my boob, stroking his thumb over my nipple. His other hand remains gripped on the back of my neck.

I can feel how hard he is against me, wanting me. We've officially touched. We really have crossed that line.

"Jacob, stop," I plead weakly, but at the same time I let out a moan as my nipples grow hard under Jacob's thumb and I feel the heat rushing in between my thighs.

"Please...stop," I pant.

"Move my hand then," Jacob whispers before biting at my neck. His hand moves from under my shirt and slides down until his fingertips approach my knicker line.

The excitement pulsates through me, my skin feels on fire, I can barely catch my breath.

"I can stop..." Jacob teases as his fingers slowly creep into my underwear.

"Don't stop," I gasp.

I part my legs slightly and allow him the room to manoeuvre into me. As soon as his fingers slide inside me, I let out a loud gasp. I feel like my whole body is throbbing, I can hear myself pulsating in my ears.

"I love feeling you," Jacob whispers before pushing his tongue inside my mouth.

Everything I wanted to talk to Jacob about, everything Sara said to me has now become jumbled and distant and a total blur. Right now, the only thing I can focus on is Jacob's fingers sliding in and out of me and how his thumb is rubbing over my most sensitive part, making me get more and more out of breath as I feel my knees getting weak and my body tightening.

"That's it…I can feel you're so close."

"Oh god…Jacob, I'm going to…."

"Yes?"

"I'm going to…" I say, out of breath, before rolling my head back as my whole-body quivers uncontrollably over Jacob's fingers.

I can barely hold myself up against the wall, but Jacob steadies me until my legs feel stronger.

Holy shit. Where the hell did that come from? Jacob smirks at me, clearly feeling quite pleased with himself to see me panting and my cheeks glowing crimson.

"Is that what you came here for?" I ask, before sitting down on the sofa and taking a swig of my vodka. I need a moment to sit down – that's exhausted me.

"No, I actually came here to talk to you. But as soon as I saw you like that…all hair messy and natural in that t-shirt, I guess my hands had other ideas. I know it's not in a hot tub like you usually prefer but needs must." He laughs, mocking me flirtatiously.

I smile at his cheekiness but the worries I have been having come flooding back.

"I think I need to talk to you too…"

"Okay…" Jacob's tone becomes more serious as he takes a seat next to me. "You first?"

"I don't know where to begin...I like you. I can't stop thinking about you and I know there's a spark between us. I can feel it all the time. But what I did, how I got your attention from my bedroom, the things I did in your hot tub, it's not me. I wish it was, because it was fun. But I'm not the type of girl who can do these things without feeling guilty the next day...and that's all I feel, all of the time. Guilt..."

I notice a look of worry and confusion come over Jacob's face the more I ramble on.

"And then I went to my cousin's wedding and we got talking and she made me realise, you're not separating. You're married. So, where does this leave me? Then today I found out my mum had an affair and all I could do was cry. Cry for my poor dad and feel so angry at my mum for hurting him..."

I can hear myself talking faster and faster as I grow stressed and emotional.

"And I don't want to be that person. I don't, Jacob. I don't want to be the one who hurts people. I'm mad at myself...I'm so mad...but I can't just be some silly affair..."

"Mia! Stop!" Jacob interrupts and puts his hands over mine gently to stop me fidgeting awkwardly.

"I came here tonight to tell you that I want to make a plan to leave Elle. I want you, Mia. You are all I want. You are all I have ever wanted."

Chapter nineteen

"I don't know…" I finally respond, sadly.

The words coming out of Jacob's mouth are exciting, they make me feel like I should be on cloud nine but I'm not. All I can think about is what my mum did to my dad and how I do not want to be that person. I can't.

"What do you mean you don't know?" Jacob demands, angrily.

"Why are you angry?"

"Because I'm okay to throw you up against a wall and make you moan my name, but I can't leave my wife and be with you? What the fuck?"

He's right. I have let so much happen, how can I try and take the moral high ground now?

"It's my fault, I know that. I can't lie to you; I want you too. But I'm not sure I can be with you this way," I say irritably before walking to the patio door for some air. I hate arguing with Jacob. The tension makes me feel as though the air is being sucked out of the room.

"Well I'm sorry that I wasn't single when you met me, Mia. I'm sorry I have spent my life trying to do the right thing and keep my family happy. I'm sorry I wasn't as brave as you and didn't start the divorce a long time ago like I should have, or better yet, I wish I had stuck with my instincts and never married her. But I did!" he yells as he stands up and follows me, frustrated.

"I did marry her; I did choose the life I thought I should have. And I'm so fucking done, Mia. I'm fucking done. So no, this won't be easy. It will be messy, it will be hard, but if it means that I get to be with you then it's worth it, right?"

"But, my mum..."

"You're not your mum, Mia! I don't even know what she did or who she fell for, but I know for a fact that this is different."

"Maybe! But she still hurt people," I snap back and I'm ready to list all the reasons why this is getting out of hand and how the idea that we can run off into the sunset is about as realistic as a Disney movie, but the knock on the door stuns me.

I quickly tiptoe to the window and peer around the drapes.

"Elle?" I whisper to myself.

Shit. I totally forgot I invited her round.

"Does Elle know you're here?" I whisper in a panic to Jacob, who looks just as surprised.

"No. I told her I wanted to go for a walk on my own."

"Did she see you come to my house?"

"I don't think so," he answers calmly.

"Fuck. Okay. Hopefully it's fine," I mumble, flustered. "There's a gate around the side of the house, through the garden, you can get out that way."

"Mia?" Elle calls through the letterbox.

"Coming!" I yell nervously.

"Go...go!" I say, as I gently push Jacob out of my patio doors.

"No. Maybe I'll tell Elle now. Maybe I'll tell her how I can't stop

115

thinking about you and how I just want to be with you. Every day."

"Jacob! Now isn't the time to give me a fucking heart attack!" I hiss. "Leave!"

"Maybe I'll tell her you keep seducing me." He smirks as he flirtatiously towers over me. God, his arrogance drives me crazy and wild all at the same time.

"Jake!" I moan desperately. My heart is racing with anxiety, my palms feel sweaty and my mouth feels suddenly so dry. Why does he enjoy teasing me like this?

"I'll go. Only if you promise to stop worrying about what your mum did and what you should and shouldn't do and just think about how happy we could be. Think about us."

His body language changes – he isn't playing games with me now; he is being sincere. His eyes are wide as he stares at me and waits for my reply. They soften, back to those puppy dog eyes that I love. He studies my face intensely, almost as if he is going to pull me in for a kiss.

"Okay! Okay!" I whisper, snapping out of his trance. "I'll think about us. I promise." And I push him out into the garden and close the patio door behind him.

He gives me one last hopeful look before turning away and disappearing down the side of the house.

I quickly rush to the mirror, running my fingers through my messy bun and try to adjust my clothes as neatly as I can. I feel like no matter what I do, somehow, she'll know. Like it's written all over my face. I feel sick.

"Coming, Elle!" I call as I rush to the front door.

She looks immaculate as always. She's wearing a yellow sleeveless top with a lilac pencil skirt and nude stilettos. Very classy and very pretty and she achieves it so effortlessly. I look like a homeless person stood next to her right now.

"Umm, Mia?" She giggles slightly. "Are you okay? You look very flustered."

"I...I... must have nodded off."

"Oh?"

"Yeah, I haven't quite been myself. I must have needed to rest."

"But you're okay now right? Because I thought we had made plans?" she asks disappointedly.

"Of course! Come in, come in!" I attempt to reassure her. "I even got us a bottle of watermelon vodka, I thought it would be nice."

"Ooh! It sounds lovely!"

I have to stop my face from screwing up as I cringe at myself. I can't believe how naturally the deceit is spilling out of me. Here I am, pouring my neighbour a vodka and lemonade and all I can think about is how ten minutes ago her husband had taken complete control of me and had me shaking underneath him.

"Been up to much?" Elle asks as I load up the ice in our glasses.

Oh, nothing much. Went to third base with your husband.

I roll my eyes at my stupid sarcastic thoughts. I hate this. I absolutely hate it.

"Not a lot really, I had a phone call with my mum earlier today and then I've just been watching movies. What about you?"

I'm so scared of slipping up or accidentally saying one of my sarcastic comments rather than just thinking them. I almost don't

117

want to talk at all.

"Ah lovely! I've been booking Cape Verde with my friend – well, assuming I go. I might cancel, I'm not sure yet."

"Really? You're going away?"

"Yeah, I think so. Shall we sit on the patio? It's still beautiful outside," Elle asks as she pulls open the patio doors and makes my heart leap into my throat.

I'm sure Jacob has had plenty of time to get out, but the fear is still there. Just in case.

A small sigh of relief comes over me as I step outside into the warm summer air and thankfully, nothing looks out of the ordinary.

"So, tell me about Cape Verde? I hear it's beautiful there," I ask curiously.

"My friend Rachael, she's getting married and she wants to do a hen weekend out there. Well, I say weekend, it's actually five days and there's ten of us altogether."

"That sounds fun! Why aren't you sure if you want to go?"

"Things are just tough at the moment," Elle answers awkwardly and takes a mouthful of her watermelon vodka. "Jacob has been distant more than usual and I'm thinking I should just stay close by. Maybe we need more marriage counselling or something."

"More?" I blurt quizzically.

"Well, yeah. We've had it off and on since we got married really. Marriage is tough. Come on Mia, you know that."

I nod and smile, agreeably. I'm mildly annoyed at the slight dig, but I let it go. I now have other things on my mind, like the thought of Elle going on a holiday without Jacob.

"It sounds to me like Cape Verde could be good for you both. You know what they say, absence makes the heart grow fonder. Maybe it's just a little space you need?"

"You really think so?"

"Absolutely!" I answer confidently. I didn't even think about encouraging her to go, it just came out of my mouth. I guess my subconscious is thinking of Jacob.

"So, when are you supposed to be going?"

"Sunday."

"Sunday? As in, three days' time?"

"Yep! I told you I wasn't sure if I wanted to go so, I left it pretty last minute. It's her second marriage anyway and you know I don't really support that kind of thing," she informs me coldly.

"Sure. I understand," I say, even though I don't agree with her views whatsoever. "But just think about the sand, sea and sangrias!"

Elle's face lights up at the thought and she smiles brightly.

"It would be fun..." she answers, looking deep in thought.

"Exactly. Plus, it'll give you and Jacob a little time to yourselves. Maybe it's what you both need," I say before I can stop myself.

"You're right! I'll go. Plus, it's not like Jacob will miss me."

"Oh yeah, that reminds me. You did seem quite upset last night. You said you were still mad at him too, about the party?"

"Yes! I'm furious, but mostly I'm annoyed that he won't even give me a good enough answer as to why he did it. Do you know how much money I spent on that party?"

I shake my head between sips of my vodka.

"Around ten thousand pounds," she announces, which makes me choke on my drink. Vodka elegantly comes flying out my nose and Elle giggles at my expense.

"Ten *thousand* pounds!?" I gawp.

"Minimum, yes. Well I had to get professional party planners in, a designer, I hired staff, bought a stack of champagne, hired caterers, it all adds up…"

"Wow, I'd have just gone down to the supermarket, got some beers in and done a barbecue in the garden with my own music playing."

"Funnily enough, Jacob suggested the same thing. Which was another argument, but never mind, I won't bore you with that."

I can't help it, but I smile as she tells me of another similarity between Jacob and me. Which reminds me how much I love being around him. Maybe five days just us, without any distractions could be amazing. Or maybe it'll be a nightmare and we'll argue and realise how stupid this all is. Either way, I'll know for sure whether this is something that'll be worth the fight.

"So, tell me more about Cape Verde?" I smile.

Chapter twenty

As I sit here and listen to Elle talk about the new bathing suit she ordered from Fendi and how she's planning on re-designing the kitchen and her desires to put an extension on the house, to make their already huge house even bigger, I begin to realise that the majority of our conversations are like this. Ninety percent of my time with Elle is spent listening to her talk, about herself, a lot. Usually I don't mind, I can be quite socially awkward and so someone taking the lead and chatting away can actually be quite refreshing, but in this instance, it's draining me.

I find myself fake laughing a lot, forcing smiles, agreeing to things I either don't understand or I don't actually agree with. I pretend to get excited about materialistic things that she gets so hyped up about, but really, I couldn't give a shit that John Lewis has a new gold and marble coffee table. And pretending I care is proving to be a lot of effort these days.

I have tried not to be rude, but I've glanced down at my phone at least half a dozen times in the last half an hour. She's been here two hours already and I have barely spoken a word.

The sun is beating down on my head, my eyes feel tired, my skin feels kind of dry. I feel like I have been sitting in the direct sun for too long and my head feels a little fuzzy. I feel like I could do with a nice shower and an early night. But Elle seems to want to discuss why she wants Jacob to agree that they need a bigger swimming pool.

It's all quite sad actually. I get a sense that she's almost addicted to spending his money. She is constantly on the lookout for ways to better their appearance. The house has to be bigger, the swimming pool longer, the kitchen needs to be refitted despite it already being very modern and luxurious. It never ends. I wonder if she is ever truly satisfied.

"Oh, and then of course I want Jacob to take me on another honeymoon. I have already asked him to sort that out, but knowing Jacob, he won't be in a rush to do it," Elle says, rolling her eyes.

"Another honeymoon?"

"Yes, well the last one was only okay. Greece is lovely but the hotel could have been better. I think it was still a five-star resort, but I want the wow factor. This time, I want to go to Santorini and have a penthouse suite, with our own infinity pool. Jacob could take a photo of me as I sit in the pool and look out into the distance, just as the sun sets. Can you imagine? That would definitely be worthy enough for my social media."

"Wow, yeah." I find myself nodding again like a bloody sheep. Everything she says I just find myself smiling and agreeing like a moron incapable of having an opinion.

"Do you have social media, Mia?" she asks inquisitively.

"I do, but I don't really use it these days. I find it's all just people becoming far too self-absorbed and fake."

"Oh. Well I love it. It's a great way to show my friends and family how well Jacob and I are doing. Here, look for yourself," she says as she passes me her phone and I look down to see hundreds of model-style images.

I feel a little tightness in my stomach, as if I'm nervous to come across photos of Elle and Jacob, posing together, living the high life. I just know I'll feel a huge wash of jealousy come over me. But to my surprise, the majority of the images are only of Elle.

It's just Elle riding a camel in the desert. Just Elle sipping on cocktails on what looks like a private beach. Another photo, of Elle on her own in a beautiful long emerald green gown on what looks like a cruise ship.

"You look lovely Elle. So happy," I say politely and hand the phone back, having gotten the gist quickly enough of how she wants her life to be seen.

"Thank you darling! We've had some amazing times; me and my Jakey."

"It certainly looks like it."

"And guess what? I wasn't going to say anything, but I found a brochure for a luxurious adult-only resort in the Bahamas! The Bahamas, Mia! Can you believe it? I know I worry about our marriage at times, and we both probably do need space every now and again, but it all boils down to the same thing. That man loves me, and he loves to surprise me," she says with a huge grin.

What the fuck? The Bahamas?

I shake my head, confused.

"Sorry Elle, I thought you said that Jacob was acting more distant than usual?"

"Yeah? He has been. But I guess he's just sorry for ruining my party and maybe he realises he was being silly about the money and he wants to treat me to something. This is what Jacob does. When things get tough, he usually books us a well-needed holiday and we come back feeling better."

My head feels worse as I listen to her words. One minute I'm picturing coming clean and running off into the sunset with Jacob and the next I'm finding out he is planning some romantic holiday with the woman he claims he wants to leave? What the fuck is this?

It's not like I can go storming over to Jacob now and start demanding answers and try to make sense of where I actually stand with him.

"Elle, I'm sorry but I've come over feeling so sick. I think I need to get to bed."

"Oh? Really?"

"Yeah, I'm sorry. I just haven't been feeling right lately. Think I just need an early night…"

"Oh okay, that's a shame, I was enjoying myself. Well okay then, I'll try and pop by before I head off to Cape Verde if you like?"

"Yeah, sure. That'll be nice," I say as I stand up and clear the drinks from the patio table. I feel quite rude, almost rushing her to finish her drink and leave but I genuinely do feel sick now.

I think it's the stress, or the thought of Jacob jetting off to a beautiful hotel with Elle and I can't cope with it all anymore. I also can't bear another moment of listening to Elle's drivel.

"Where was the watermelon vodka from? I might have to go and get some."

"I got it in ASDA," I answer as I open the front door for her.

"Oh. That'll be why I never saw it before. I haven't ever stepped foot in one of those supermarkets. I usually just stick to the boutique food shops where I can get mine and Jacob's favourites."

I refrain from commenting on yet another insult and attempt to smile gracefully.

"Here, you can have the rest," I say as I grab the bottle of vodka from the kitchen side and hand it to her.

"Aw, Mia, you're so kind."

"You're welcome. Goodnight," I respond before closing the front door behind her and letting out a sigh of relief.

Fuck.

I feel tears rushing to my eyes and I'm so angry that I'm crying over Jacob *again* that it makes me even more upset.

Fucking Bahamas. Fucking Elle. Fuck this.

I rush up to my bedroom and slam the door behind me. I feel sick. What am I a part of? I'm not even sure I know anymore.

Just as I turn to get into bed, I see movement in the corner of my eye. It's Jacob up at his office window. He raises his hand to wave as he continues to stare at me. My eyes are too watery with tears, but I think he is smiling. I shake my head before turning my back and diving into my bed.

Listen to your head, Mia. Forget Jacob. You're going to get hurt.

Chapter twenty-one

I could count on one hand the amount of times I have ever gone out for drinks on my own. It's not something I like to do. I don't mind my own company, but I feel awkward sitting at a bar, alone.

Despite this, I'm applying the last of my make-up and waiting for my taxi into town. There's a new Cuban bar and to celebrate the grand opening, they're doing half-price cocktails all night.

Today has more or less been a write-off. I woke up with puffy eyes, a horrible feeling of emptiness in my stomach and feeling hugely anxious overall.

I have tried to do all the things I could think of to make myself feel better, including a long soak in the tub, watching some more of my favourite movies and listening to my most upbeat playlist. But nothing has changed how unsure and fed up I feel.

That's when it hit me. I moved to a new area and the only people I have socialised with are my neighbours. No wonder I've allowed myself to crush over Jacob and get so caught up in their failed marriage. I haven't pushed myself to meet other locals and I really ought to. Tonight, I'm going to try and meet new people and maybe I'll start to see things in a whole different light. Jacob can go to the Bahamas for all I care. If he thinks I'm just going to be a bit of fun for a while and then when he is done and wants to work on his marriage, he can just drop me and whisk his wife away to some glamorous hotel, then he has another think coming.

Thankfully, getting dressed up and putting on a fresh face of make-up has made me feel better. I'm wearing a black satin shirt dress and a belt; I bought it in a sale last year but never had the chance to wear it, until now.

The taxi beeps loudly outside my driveway and I grab my clutch bag and lip-gloss and head out of the door and towards the car. It's still quite light outside, despite it being nearly eight thirty.

Just as I open the car door, I hear a similar sound behind me. It's Jacob's car. The black Range Rover that he typically favours over his other two cars.

He spots me almost instantly as he appears from around the corner. His eyes go wide as he looks me up and down, admiring the satin dress clinging against my curves, but his expression quickly changes to confusion and almost panic as I disappear into the taxi, closing my door promptly behind me.

The taxi journey is only ten minutes but the closer we get; the more nerves seem to take hold of me. I can't help but worry that I might just look like a complete loser in a bar drinking alone. But I guess it's too late to turn back now.

"Where are you going looking like that?" The message flashes up on my phone screen.

It's Jacob. He must have found me on social media. I open the private inbox and read over his words again and again. I start typing but before I can even think of a decent reply, I delete it and put my phone back in my bag.

I don't have to justify myself to him. I don't have to answer his questions. The more I think about it, the angrier I become which makes me pull my phone out of my bag and message back.

"What has it got to do with you?" I click send and my heart begins to race as almost instantly I can see Jacob is typing back by the dots on the screen.

"What? Why are you being like that?" he answers quickly.

I roll my eyes at his arrogance. As if I'm being like anything when he is the one booking romantic trips to the fucking Bahamas. Eurgh. I swear if I hear the word Bahamas one more time, or even think it, I'm going to scream. I am so fed up now and Jacob messaging me has just made it a hundred times worse.

"Mia? Are you going on a fucking date?" My phone lights up with his words again as another message invades my screen. This time I throw it back in my bag and tell myself that it's time to go and enjoy my night and not answer any more of his annoying messages.

The Cuban bar is packed when I arrive which fills me with anxiety and dread. Luckily, I spot a free bar stool at the far end of the bar and I quickly rush over to it before it gets taken.

"Welcome to Havana's, what can I get you?" the friendly barmaid asks me.

I didn't expect her to come over so quickly. I haven't even had the chance to check over the menu. Everything looks amazing, so many tropical looking cocktails around me. I love the atmosphere in here already, despite it being busy.

"Erm, I'm not sure. What do you recommend?"

"Well, we have the all-time favourite Sex on the beach, or we have a new cocktail which is going down a storm called the Blue Bahama?"

Of course, it would be. Fucking Bahamas.

"I'll have a Sex on the beach please, to start," I say with a forced smile.

I can feel my phone vibrating in my bag. I haven't even looked but I somehow know it's Jacob calling me through my social media.

The waitress brings over a tall glass of a pink cocktail with umbrellas and neon straws coming out of it. The rim is frosted in sugar and there's a wedge of lime on the side. I have to stop myself from grabbing my phone and taking a typical photo to share online. I hope it tastes as good as it looks.

"And here's your free shot of tequila," the friendly girl says.

"Oh?"

"Yep, free shots with all cocktails tonight. Enjoy!" She smiles before disappearing to the other side of the bar.

I knock the tequila down quickly which kicks the back of my throat and nearly makes me cough. I can feel the liquid burning my chest as I swallow it. I take a few sips of my cocktail to ease it, which tastes delicious.

I'm not entirely sure what to do now. I'm here, I'm dressed up, I have my cocktail and now I'm...bored.

Looking around me, nearly everyone here has come out in groups. There's a group of six or seven girls standing at the bar opposite me, all dressed up with sashes on and learner plates. Obviously, a hen party. They look like they're having lots of fun.

There are a few couples too, but I try to pay less attention to them.

I pull my phone out of my bag and turn it off. The constant vibrating is annoying me. I can see Jacob has tried calling me eight times already and another call comes through just as I switch it off.

I peruse the cocktail menu, enjoying all the brilliant names of the various different drinks. Coconut chaos, Wave crasher, White shark and a few rude ones which makes me smirk. Naughty knicker-dropper, Pink nipple and Sunset blowjob just to name a few.

"Can I get you another?" the barmaid says as she heads back over to me.

"Oh, sure. I'll have a Pink nipple please."

I sip on the rest of my Sex on the beach whilst I excitedly wait for my Pink nipple. Cocktail menus are definitely for adults what pick'n'mix are for children. It's far too much fun choosing different flavours to try, especially when they all come in these fancy different colours and flamboyant glasses.

"One Pink nipple and another tequila," the barmaid says as she lays out the drinks in front of me.

I throw back my second shot of tequila which burns less than the first one, but I still need a sip of my cocktail afterwards to cool down my chest. The Pink nipple is absolutely delicious. It tastes like strawberry mostly with a hint of mint. Not what I expected but so refreshing.

"Excuse me?" A masculine voice startles me.

I swing around in my bar stool to see a tall blond guy smiling back at me.

"Yes?"

"I think you owe me a drink."

"Erm, and why is that?" I laugh nervously.

"Because when I saw you, I dropped mine," he answers.

I shake my head and burst out laughing.

"Okay, okay. It was terrible and cheesy but at least I made you smile. Which is the first time you have since you walked through those doors," he says softly before taking a seat next to me.

"I'm Daniel."

"Mia," I answer politely.

"So, Mia. Can I buy you another cocktail?"

"Sure," I smile. "That'll be nice."

Chapter twenty-two

Daniel is handsome but not really my type. He seems too up-market for me. His blond hair is neatly combed, and he is wearing a collared t-shirt, I think its designer but I'm not sure. He is very slim, the complete opposite of Jacob, who is more muscular and broader. He does have a cheesy grin though and gorgeous green eyes which almost make him look exotic. To be honest I feel like he would perfectly suit Elle. He would complement her *perfect* appearance.

"Two Pink nipples please," Daniel asks the barmaid when he finally gets her attention.

I smirk at the thought of a man sipping on a Pink nipple with umbrellas and pink straws.

"What?" Daniel laughs as he catches my smirk.

"Nothing. It's just not the manliest of drinks."

"Well I can't let you drink these cocktails on your own, now can I?"

"I wouldn't mind if you ordered a beer. Unless of course it's the pretty pink umbrellas you're really after," I playfully tease, which makes him laugh again.

Our drinks arrive quickly, and I giggle as I watch Daniel sip on his girly drink. He pretends to get all offended at my giggling which makes me laugh more. So far, he is proving to be good company, despite his cheesy chat-up lines.

"So, Daniel, what do you do for a living?"

"If I tell you, you can't laugh, okay?"

"Okay..." I answer, amused already.

"I'm a farmer."

"What's funny about that?"

"Nothing! But you'd be surprised by the number of women I have met who find it funny and then ask me about my combine harvester."

I almost choke on my drink as I burst out laughing.

"See! Now you're laughing!" Daniel giggles and jokingly glares at me.

"Sorry! I don't even know why I'm laughing. I guess it's just the thought of you on a combine harvester!"

"No... no... that's not the image I want you to have of me..."

"Okay, Daniel. What image would you like me to have?" I ask as I lean forward with my head resting on my hand to indicate that I'm listening intently.

"Like, a sexy masculine farmer, taking care of animals and trekking through my fields in my manly wellies."

"Manly wellies?" I ask before letting out another chuckle.

"Right then! Come on, you tell me what you do for a living Mia and I bet it won't be at all sexy and I can mock you for that."

"Fine..." I answer and I try to compose myself. "I'm a sports journalist."

Daniel stares at me intently for a second before a huge smile spreads across his face.

"Okay, you win. That's kind of hot."

"It is?"

"Yeah! Now I'm imagining you in like a football shirt and it just...works."

I giggle again at his statement.

"And what is sexy about a football shirt?"

"Usually nothing. But the thought of you in one...with nothing else on, it's a turn on."

"Oh!" I gasp as I jokingly nudge his arm. "Are you trying to flirt with me Daniel?"

"Perhaps," he answers with a small smile and takes another sip of his Pink nipple.

The conversation is flowing effortlessly. Initially he wasn't my type but one thing I'm already drawn to is how he is so uncomplicated. He has no wife, no girlfriend, no children, nothing. He just works on his farm, spends weekends watching football and hanging out with his mates and that's it. Being with somebody like Daniel would be totally easy and stress-free.

"Okay, it's my turn," Daniel says as he picks up the menu.

Between us we have created a new game. We take it in turns to close our eyes and run our finger over the cocktails until the other person shouts stop and whatever we land on is our next drink.

"Stop!" I giggle.

"Okay...ooh, looks like we're having two Sunset blow-jobs!" Daniel proudly announces with his huge cheeky grin.

I roll my eyes playfully but giggle as I sip the last drop of cocktail through my straw. I'm beginning to lose track of how many we've had now. I think we are about to have our sixth along with, yet another tequila shot. My head definitely feels a lot lighter and I'm giggling more and more, which is a sure enough sign I'm getting tipsy.

The bar has slowly started to empty now and there's only a couple more tables being occupied, and we are now the only ones seated at the bar.

"What time is it?" I ask out loud as I fish for my phone in my bag.

I don't think Daniel hears me though as he is busy ordering our cocktails. It's quite hard to focus on my bright screen as I switch my phone back on, but I think it's just gone eleven.

My phone starts to buzz in my hand as message after message comes through.

"Fuck, Mia. You're driving me crazy. Talk to me," one of them reads as it pops up on my screen.

I shake my head and throw it back into my bag. I can't be bothered with Jacob anymore tonight. How dare he say I drive him crazy when he is playing me like a game.

"Cheers!" Daniel says as he hands me another tequila.

I try to smile as I take it and instantly throw it back; this time, I feel no burn at all. Now I know I'm drunk.

"What's wrong?"

"Nothing, why?" I mutter, confused.

"Well you've been giggling all night but since looking at your phone you look...I don't know...sad?"

I contemplate offloading the whole story to Daniel for a minute but a quick image of me rambling on in my drunken state comes to my mind and I decide it's not an attractive look to tell him I've been lusting over my neighbour and now I'm jealous he is taking his annoying wife to the sodding Bahamas.

"I... I don't know. I just realised it's getting late and I guess I should be getting home soon."

"Do you want company?" Daniel asks as he leans into me and slides his arm around my waist.

My heart is saying no, I want to go home alone, but for some reason I'm already nodding. Just as Daniel plants a kiss on my lips.

I'm immediately disappointed when my heart doesn't race, and my skin doesn't feel like it's on fire the way it does when Jacob touches me. Maybe it's the alcohol. Maybe I have numbed myself to it.

When he pulls away, I see our untouched fresh cocktails out of the corner of my eye. I grab mine quickly and start knocking it back, which seems to impress and amuse Daniel. I know if I sit here and wait too long, I'll end up talking myself out of this. And I can't do that. I have to move on. Jacob's true intentions were made clear to me the second Elle announced their trip.

Daniel picks up his drink and knocks it back along with me. When I've finished chugging at the last gulp, I slam my glass down onto the bar and take Daniel by the hand.

We leave the bar quickly and I hurry us over to the taxi rank. The second we both get into the back seat; Daniel's hand is already wandering up my inner thigh. I sit back and pull him close to me by his shirt as I slide my tongue over his.

I try to calm myself down when I catch the taxi driver glancing at us in the mirror. It makes me giggle; I feel like a teenager again right now. This new carefree fun is exactly what I have needed.

Before I know it, the taxi driver has pulled into my driveway. Daniel pays him despite me putting up a bit of an argument, but I admire how gentlemanly he is. Daniel keeps his hands on me as I stagger to the front door. It's dark and I'm struggling to get my key into the lock.

"Shhh," I drunkenly say to the keys just after I drop them on the floor. I can't help but giggle at myself.

I bend down and feel around for the keys and feel Daniel's hand slide up my dress and caress me from behind. I find the keys and quickly attempt again to open the door.

This time I manage to get the key in correctly. The second the door opens, Daniel grabs me, picks me up and shoves me passionately against the wall. I wrap my legs tightly around his waist and groan as he slides his tongue over my cleavage.

"You're so hot," Daniel mumbles as he pulls my dress up over my hips.

I'm not even sure now if I want to be doing this but it seems too late to stop him. I keep my eyes tightly shut as I feel Daniel unbuckle the belt on his jeans.

"What the FUCK, Mia?" I hear the deep growl come from behind Daniel.

Fuck.

The hallway light pings on and I see Jacob standing there, gawping. He stares at me in disbelief before looking Daniel up and down and now his eyes have turned sharp and wild. His jaw is clenched.

Oh shit.

I know what's coming.

"Jacob!" I gasp.

Chapter twenty-three

I watch as the skin around Jacob's knuckles turns white the harder, he clenches his fist.

"Move the fuck away from her," he demands, and he takes a step towards Daniel.

"Don't, Jacob!" I shout and stand in front of him confrontationally. I know just how quickly his temper can turn, I remember the fight outside his house only too well and I won't allow him to do that here.

Daniel looks surprised but not too phased by Jacob's threats.

"What's going on? I don't understand. Mia, I thought you said you were single?"

"I am single!" I protest.

"Then who the fuck is this guy?"

"He's...he's my neighbour."

"Your neighbour?" Daniel scoffs and stares at Jacob as if he's insane.

For a moment I'm convinced Jacob is about to lunge at Daniel and beat the crap out of him just for that sarcastic laugh alone, but to my surprise he turns to me instead.

"Is that it, Mia? Is that all I am?" he bellows in my direction. "Well? Answer me!"

"I don't have to answer any of your questions! If I wanted to, don't you think I would have replied to you tonight? Just go home Jacob. Back to Elle!"

I realise how loud I'm talking. I tried to start off so calmly but by the end I'm practically screaming in his face.

I have so many conflicting emotions and I hate him being here. He confuses me so easily. Being with Daniel was easy but now Jacob is here, and everything is complicated again.

"There's no fucking way I'm leaving you with *him,* you have to be joking!" Jacob yells again.

"For your information, I've been having the best night I have had in ages with Daniel," I say, purposely antagonising him. Although I'm slightly scared of how angry he is getting, and I'm worried he'll lash out at Daniel, but I want him to feel shit just like I have been.

"Bullshit!" Jacob fires back arrogantly. "That's why you looked bored up against that wall, is it?"

I shoot him a glare. He's right and I hate it. I wasn't exactly seeing fireworks with Daniel, but I wish he didn't have to call me out on it.

"Is that why your eyes were shut? Probably trying to picture me instead," Jacob continues to push, arrogantly.

"You know nothing! At least Daniel doesn't come with an alcoholic, money-grabbing, selfish wife like yours!"

"Yeah and you've never used *that* to your advantage, have you? You've never supplied her with alcohol, have you!?"

I instantly cringe at the memory.

"Oh please! Like she needs encouraging!"

"Mia...maybe I should leave, we can do this another time, if you want?" Daniel hesitantly interrupts.

"Pffft," Jacob sarcastically chuckles. "No fucking way."

Daniel is already heading for the front door before I even have a chance to try and persuade him otherwise. Jacob has definitely killed the mood.

"I'll call you..." I politely answer.

"No, she won't," Jacob childishly adds.

Daniel turns back to offer a smile, albeit reluctantly, and somehow, I already know I won't be hearing from him ever again. Jacob is enough to scare anybody off when he is in one of these moods.

As soon as the door closes behind him, I'm barely given a second before another question is fired at me.

"Well? What the fuck is going on?"

"I'm not in the mood Jacob! Why don't you go home, back to your wife? Isn't she wondering where you are right now?"

"She's passed out on the sofa as usual," he mumbles and for a second, a wash of empathy for him comes over me. "Plus, I need answers. I'm not going anywhere."

He is being relentless.

I awkwardly adjust my dress, making sure it's pulled down and covering me before I head for the kitchen. Jacob closely follows behind.

His breathing is still heavy like he could kick off at any moment and he keeps doing that thing where he clenches his jaw. God it makes him look sexy. Which I try to ignore.

I'm not sure what to do with myself, but without thinking I'm grabbing a bottle of wine from the fridge.

"Haven't you had enough tonight?"

"Shouldn't you be saying that to your wife?" I snap. But immediately feel guilty for the harsh dig.

"Fuck Mia! What's gotten into you? Why are you playing these games?"

"'Me, playing games? That's rich! Considering you're the one planning a secret getaway to the fucking Bahamas!"

"Bahamas? How the hell do you know about that?" Jacob asks, confused, his voice finally softening.

"Your wife told me! She couldn't tell me quickly enough! She told me all about how you often book little breaks away to fix your circus of a marriage!" I scream and tears fill my eyes.

Oh shit. No Mia, don't. Don't cry. Hold it back.

"*Mia*?" Jacob steps towards me, closing the space between us.

His thumb comes up to my cheek and he gently wipes the tear away that has fallen.

"Please don't. Please don't touch me. This has gotten too deep. I'm scared of how I'm feeling now. And then you booked the Bahamas...and that's just more than I can bear. I thought...I thought it was me you wanted. Why would you do that?"

"Mia, you've got it all so wrong," Jacob says so gently whilst he continues to cup my cheek; the warmth of his palm is comforting.

I gaze up at his eyes and they're so different than they were ten minutes ago. They're no longer wild or angry, but soft and understanding.

"Mia, listen to me. I booked the Bahamas a couple of days ago when I decided I wanted to start the shit storm that will come when I tell Elle I want a divorce. I was worried about all this causing you stress and I didn't want you to lose sight of us. So, I thought I'd book a break. Just you and me. I just wanted to protect you and give you some space away from here."

He brings his other hand up to my cheek and gently pulls me close to place a kiss on my lips. It's the gentlest kiss, almost as if I'm fragile and he needs to be careful with me. I open my mouth slightly and welcome his tongue as he slides it over mine. My heart beats hard against my chest. Jacob runs his fingers through my hair before gripping the ends and pulling my head back slightly as he slides his tongue in harder and kisses me passionately.

"Jake..." I moan as goosebumps rush over my entire body.

I love how he brings his hands down to my waist and pulls me in so tightly; I feel like he'll never let go of me.

"Mia?" he whispers and pulls away just enough to stare into my eyes. "How do you not see by now that I've fallen for you?"

Chapter twenty-four

It took me so long to fall asleep last night. After Jacob left, all I could think about were his words. How he has *fallen* for me. I can't quite believe how quickly this has all happened. One minute, I was just the new neighbour to the suburbs, ready to throw myself into my work and quietly spend my evenings alone with a glass of red and my new friend, Puss. The very last thing that was on my mind was falling for a new man. Particularly a married one. I guess the saying is true, things really do happen when you least expect them to.

I woke up this morning feeling so different from yesterday. Well, almost. I feel great but also a little foolish after my antics with Daniel. Now that Jacob has made me understand it was all a case of having my wires crossed, I feel quite silly that I allowed the whole thing to unravel the way that it did. Especially for Daniel's sake – he was actually a really decent guy and didn't deserve to be caught up in our drama.

I can't lie though, Jacob's protective nature at times can be quite a turn on. The way his face was wild with anger when he saw my legs wrapped around another man, it was intense. I can feel this pent-up energy growing between us and last night I wanted nothing more than for Jacob to take me to bed. But neither of us will allow it. It's strange, nothing we have done has been exactly innocent but when it comes to sex, I know we are both waiting. For the right time, or at least a better time. A time when Jacob is officially separated, perhaps.

It really is quite incredible how much my mood has improved

since sorting things with Jacob. Rather than dragging myself out of bed, I'm up fresh and have all the energy to give this entire house a good clean. The spring is well and truly back in my step and I'm practically singing at the top of my lungs as I give the house a vacuum.

"Mia!?! I really need a wee!" I hear an all-too-familiar voice calling through my letterbox as I turn off the vacuum. I hurry downstairs.

"Sara?" I say, surprised to see my cousin as she rushes past me the second, I open the door.

"Can't talk! Full bladder!" she shouts before disappearing into my bathroom.

I smirk at the thought of Sara frantically knocking on my door which I couldn't hear over the vacuum noise.

I wish she had given me a slight heads up that she was coming though – I can't help but feel a little uncomfortable in my old white vest and my pink pyjama shorts with my hair shoved up high in a messy bun. A shower and some appropriate clothing were next on my list after all the cleaning and vacuuming.

"God, that was a close call!" Sara smiles as she reappears in the hallway. "Way too much coffee this morning!"

"This is very out of the blue?"

"I know, I had to come by. I was worried about you after my wedding. I got the feeling I upset you a bit."

I pull at my clothes awkwardly. Sara did make me feel a bit fed up and it was annoying to have her burst my bubble. But I'm not good at honestly saying how I feel.

"It was fine. Don't worry about it," I finally answer. "Cup of tea? I'll put the kettle on."

"Good! So, you're not upset with me?"

"No. It's fine, honestly. I get you were saying it all from a good place. It was just a little difficult to hear, especially because you don't know Jacob like I do. I promise, this isn't just some game to him."

I try to say it assertively, so she knows not to throw more questions my way. But whilst I make our drinks, I notice her staring at me blankly.

"Oh. Okay," she finally adds hesitantly. "So, he's left his wife then has he?"

"Well, no. Not yet," I answer honestly. "It's happening very soon though."

"Oh, Mia."

"Sara, please don't start," I plead. "I can't hear all of this again. You don't know him."

"I just saw him, outside. I'm not even sure what you see in him."

"Did you?" My voice goes all high pitched and squeaky.

"Yeah, watering his plants. In his straw hat."

"Huh? A straw hat!? Oh! No! That's Mr Jenkins!" I manage to say before roaring with laughter. "Jesus, Sara! The man is in his late sixties and happily married to his wife."

"Oh!" Sara giggles. "I'm quite relieved I must say. So, where does Jacob live?"

"Jacob *is* my neighbour; he just lives opposite."

"Oh, cool. Why don't you invite him over, I'd love to meet him," Sara says between sips of her tea.

Somehow, I know instantly that was a completely disingenuous comment.

"I can't just invite him over. Elle will be there." I shrug awkwardly.

"Elle, as in his wife?"

"Yes, Sara, his wife." I sigh, growing frustrated with her again.

"I'm sorry, I don't mean to annoy you. I really don't. I'm just worried. This isn't very, well, very you."

"I fell for someone. It happens every day. How is that not me?"

"You know what I mean! He is off the market. This isn't something you would usually entertain."

"I'm sorry that not everyone can fall in love at school and go on to marry their childhood sweetheart, Sara," I snap defensively.

"Wow. Okay," Sara responds with a sarcastic tone.

"I just don't believe that everything in life is that black and white anymore. Just because I haven't fallen for someone in a conventional way that suits your standards doesn't mean I haven't met someone wonderful. Wonderful for me, anyway."

"Okay fine," she huffs. "I love you to bits, but I don't think I can support this."

"Then leave," I reply sternly, which makes Sara's face screw up in shock.

"Mia?"

"I'm sick of it. You don't have to agree with my choices, but they *are* my choices and I won't spend the rest of my life explaining myself."

"This is going to end in tears," Sara warns firmly as she stands up ready to leave.

"I'm a big girl. I can handle it."

"Don't say I didn't warn you then. When you realise, he isn't worth all the hurt and trouble the pair of you will cause, give me a call."

I hate how her tone is so patronising. Like I'm some clueless teenager and she's some wise superior person with the perfect life. I can't find any words to respond to her again, but I think my face says it all.

"Err, hello?" Jacob startles us as he appears in the kitchen doorway. "Sorry, the front door was open. Is this a bad time?"

"No, no, not at all. My cousin was just leaving," I try to say calmly and force Jacob a smile.

"Yeah. I was just leaving. It seems me and Mia have nothing left to talk about anymore," Sara mutters as she shakes her head and grabs her bag off the side.

The look she gives Jacob makes me cringe with embarrassment. She shoots him a glare with nothing but judgement and disgust in her expression.

I can see from Jacob's face that he has worked out why there is an atmosphere. I told him before what Sara had said at her wedding when we were arguing. Only because it was weighing so heavily on my mind and I needed his reassurance.

"I'm just going to jump in the shower quickly Jake, can you wait for a minute or is it urgent?"

"I'll wait," he responds with a reassuring smile.

I offer Sara a small smile as a peace offering before turning my back and heading up the stairs.

"Just remember what I said, Mia," she calls after me.

The second I'm in my bedroom and on my own I let out the biggest sigh. That was awful and awkward and ridiculously stressful. Did she just come here to make me feel like the world's shittiest person?

I peer out of my window and watch her as she heads for her car. God knows when I'll see her again now.

"Sara..." I hear Jacob quietly call as he takes a few steps behind her.

Sara turns on her heel to face him with all the attitude of a stroppy child about to throw a tantrum.

What's he doing? Please Jacob, don't waste your breath, I think to myself. She's stubborn, she'll never change her opinion on how we have gotten started, no matter how much he pleads our case.

Wait. What's happening?

Sara's face has dropped and now looks serious and frightened. My eyes drop down to see Jacob has a hold of her elbow and it looks as though he is holding her tightly because Sara's body looks so stiff.

He leans toward to her and I think he is whispering into her ear. By Sara's reaction it can't be good because she grows anxious and unsettled with each second that goes by.

Jacob eventually let's go of her arm and she takes a step back. I say eventually, it's probably only seconds but the intensity makes it seem so much longer. She gives him a quick glance, but I can tell she's too uneasy to hold eye contact with him.

She turns back on her heel and picks up the pace as she hurriedly climbs into her car and within a split second she has sped away.

What on earth did he say?

Chapter twenty-five

I'm in and out of the shower in record time. I'm eager to get downstairs and quiz Jacob on what he just said to Sara, but I had to shower first. I'm still not overly comfortable with him seeing me so dressed down.

Droplets of water keep trickling down my back from my freshly washed hair, but I don't have time to waste drying it. I throw on a pretty white tea party dress and grab another towel for my hair and head downstairs.

"Your little friend is back." Jacob smiles, gesturing towards Puss who has appeared at my patio door. As usual.

I glance at Puss but I'm too intrigued by what I saw to pay too much attention.

"What happened outside?" I press curiously.

"Well lots of things happen outside; can you be more specific?" he replies jokily to make me smile. But I'm not feeling in a jokey mood.

"With Sara?"

"Oh! That. I just had a quick word. That's all."

"Wha-what? Why!?" My voice suddenly becomes high pitched and squeaky again. Seemingly a trend for today.

"Relax, I just told her to back off. That was all."

"Jake..." I roll my eyes so hard I'm surprised they're not stuck to the back of my head. "Why did you do that? She was already pretty annoyed at me with what I'm doing. Well, what we're doing."

"Yeah I know. I heard her pissy little attitude as soon as I got to the front door. I don't need her stressing you out and making you doubt us."

"I do agree with that, but I just think she's worried, that's all."

"Look, I know this isn't exactly a fairy-tale beginning, but you deserve better than having some goody goody judging your every choice. You don't need to be listening to all that," Jacob says firmly. I always know when he is wound up because he clenches his jaw. Frustratingly it's also one of the things I find irresistible about him.

"Okay, fine." I sigh, backing down a lot quicker than I had anticipated. Damn that clenched jaw. "But in future, please just let me deal with Sara. I know she's a hot head, but she means well."

I get the feeling Jacob isn't used to being told what to do but he reluctantly nods his head in agreement anyway.

"Come here," he demands with a smile as his eyes drift up and down my body.

I take a few steps closer to where he is perched on the edge of my dining chair and as soon as I'm within reach, he gently pulls the bottom of my short dress to guide me in so that I'm standing in between his legs.

"You look absolutely beautiful, Mia," he whispers as his hands clasp tightly around the back of my legs and he looks up at me and studies my face. Almost as if he is appreciating every line and every feature that makes me, me.

"You're not so bad yourself," I say softly with a smirk across my lips.

To be fair, he does look particularly good today. I can tell he has just come from his morning gym workout because he is in much more relaxed clothing, just a white t-shirt with short, cuffed sleeves, showing off his big arms, and a pair of light grey jogger shorts. I love this look.

Gently, Jacob places a kiss onto my stomach through my dress. I can feel his warm lips through the fabric, and I must admit it's making my heart rate speed up a little.

I look down to see Jacob bending his head down lower and I feel the kisses pushing against my hip bone and eventually towards my inner thigh.

I gasp at the excitement which I can tell makes him laugh a little because I feel his hot breath suddenly against my skin.

Every part of my body suddenly feels extra sensitive. I can feel my skin heating up and my heartbeat beginning to thump so loudly I can feel it all over my body. Particularly between my legs.

I close my eyes and my jaw drops open slightly as I feel Jacob's tongue slide over my opening through my knickers.

"Fuck," I whimper as I let my head roll back in enjoyment, allowing myself to fully sink into this moment.

I use one hand to steady myself carefully against the table and run the other hand through his hair and grip it tightly whilst he continues to swipe his tongue over me.

My knickers are getting wetter with each stroke of his tongue but at this point I really couldn't care less.

His hands travel up to my bum cheeks and he grips them hard in his palms as he continues pushing his tongue against me until I moan. I thrust my hips a little so that I'm pushing myself harder onto his mouth. My knees are buckling under all his teasing, but

I feel his grip steady me.

My fast breathing turns to more of a pant and I know I'm getting close.

Unexpectedly, I stop feeling his tongue against me and instead the gentle kisses on my inner thigh resume.

"That's enough for one day."

"Huh?" I manage to say through flustered breaths.

"That's why I came over. To invite you to spend the weekend with me whilst Elle is away. But first I wanted to give you an idea of what's to come and hopefully you won't say no."

He looks so smug as he leans back into the chair and watches how red and dishevelled I now am.

"You're a prick," I mumble as I catch my breath and take a step back to pull down my dress and compose myself.

"I take it that's a yes?" He smirks, confident enough that I'll agree.

"Okay, fine, I will. I would love to in fact. But after that little stunt, I will absolutely not be tempted again, and we will definitely keep it to a PG version this weekend."

If anything, that just makes Jacob's eyes gleam as he shakes his head at me and lets out a chuckle.

"I'll believe it when I see it."

"Eurgh! You're so cocky!" I sigh in frustration and throw a sofa pillow at him, which just makes him chuckle harder.

"Okay, okay. This'll be interesting. We'll see who caves first," he says with an overconfident grin and heads for the front door.

"Did anyone ever tell you that you can be incredibly arrogant?"

"Funnily enough, yes. Has anyone ever told you that you're a lot of fun in a hot tub?" he fires back with a telling smile that just makes me want to throw something harder at him.

God, he drives me crazy.

"Get out!" I playfully yell.

Just as I see the front door about to close, he pops his head back round.

"Don't forget your bikini!" he simply says with a wink, before closing the door.

Chapter twenty-six: Jacob's point of view

I'm half revelling in the release with Mia and half raging inside over that *fucking* Sara. Who does she think she is? How dare she think that she has any clue about me or my relationship with Mia?

I know it's not exactly conventional. But who is she to judge? I can't have Mia being fed doubts about us. I can't lose her. She's been the first thing in my life that has given me any sort of rush. When I'm with her, my adrenaline is sky high, but in every good way imaginable.

I can't have Sara putting her two pence in. I already know how fucked up this situation is. I know that at any given moment, Mia could realise how crazy this is. The thought of being with a married man and the guilt for Elle could take over anytime and she might not want me anymore. Before I have the chance to fix everything, she might turn her back on it. The very thought makes me feel a rush of feelings I haven't felt before. I don't know whether I want to throw up, punch a wall or down half a bottle of whiskey to numb some of those feelings. I'm not used to them.

Ever since I met Mia, she's become my escape. My escape from who I am and the shitty life I have created for myself. I catch myself wondering about her throughout the day. I wonder what she's doing, if she's happy, if she's thinking of me. I count down the minutes until I can find some bullshit excuse to get out of the house and go and see her, even if it's just for a few minutes.

She's the closest thing to love I have ever experienced. My escape. My Mia.

Fuck. I cringe at myself with these thoughts that race around my head. I read a book once called *How to get the life you deserve,* and it described love as a weakness. I never understood that until now. This is probably the most vulnerable I have ever been in my life and I fucking hate it. But I also need it. Want it. Ache for it. For her.

As I approach the house my heart almost sinks at the thought of walking back into my home with Elle there. I hate myself for those thoughts. It's not her fault, really. She was just as much pushed into this marriage as I was.

My dad always said that I should marry a woman who would look good standing next to me at my work functions but who was disciplined and educated enough to understand how she should act and not show me up. And that's around the time I was introduced to Elle.

My mum said that love comes in time. That it is something you work on in a marriage. I hadn't experienced love at that point in my life and so I just assumed what my mum said would be right. Although to be honest I don't even recall wanting it. I can't say I cared for it. I wanted to be successful and that was it.

"What's taken you so long? Did you get my suitcase from the garage?" Elle says with her arms folded and a displeased look on her face as she stares down at me from the staircase.

Fuck.

"I-I... I couldn't see it. The lights in the garage aren't working. I've come back to grab a torch and then I'll be able to get it," I manage to reply with the first excuse that pops into my mind.

Elle sighs and her eyes look me up and down as if I've suddenly become such a nuisance to her and her plans.

"Okay, fine. When you get back, we need to discuss money."

"Money?"

"Yes. Money. I need some for Cape Verde. I'm completely maxed out and…"

"Hang on, completely maxed out?" I interrupt her, feeling my temper rise. This isn't the first time she's done this.

"Yes." She responds in such an arrogant manner that I can feel myself wanting to kick off, but I restrain myself. It gets us nowhere. This is who she is, she knows no better.

"Elle, I give you enough money, a very attractive amount of money each month to make sure you are more than covered for all the lunch dates and shopping sprees you need. *How* can you need more?"

"Oh, for god's sake Jacob!" she huffs impatiently as if my question is totally unreasonable. "I hired a private yacht for Cape Verde. Elouise wanted to just hire a day boat, but can you imagine trying to get a decent photo for my social media on one of those things!?"

She throws her head back and laughs as if what she has just said should be absolutely obvious. I know she expects me to laugh too, and perhaps at one point in my life I would have. But my god, I know better now.

"A yacht doesn't cost that much. What else?"

"Birthdays, Jacob! You wouldn't know because you leave it down to me to buy for all our friends and family. Kirsty just had her fortieth and she's going through a Prada phase," she replies with her face screwed up as if Prada is totally beneath her.

"You don't even like Kirsty," I say, trying my best to understand her.

"Oh Jacob!" She groans agitatedly. "I'm not going to turn up at her party with anything less than the best. You should know me by now."

I do know her. That's the fucking problem. She's become everything I hate in my own life, a reflection of everything I have fought to become but absolutely not who I want to be. It's not her fault, really. She's been moulded this way; she knows no better and perhaps there is the perfect match out there for her, someone who is just as driven by status and social media as she is. But it's not me. I wonder if she knows that it's not me either. Are we both just hanging on to this because it's expected of us?

"I'll go get the suitcase," I respond flatly before grabbing the torch from a drawer and heading back out.

I don't need the torch and I know exactly where the suitcase is. But instead of getting it, I pull out an old coffee table and sit on it, in the middle of the dark garage. I sit and think about my life. How I got into this. How I so desperately want to get out of it.

I think about how I feel when I'm with Mia. How different I become. Money doesn't mean a lot for Mia. She doesn't get excited over the new Cartier watch or the new Louis Vuitton season. Her face lights up when some bloody stray cat takes a shine to her and strolls through her patio doors to see her. Her eyes sparkle when some big sporting event comes up and she gets to write about it. Her heart races when she touches my body. I've felt it. She sees me, over the bullshit and the money and the overly decorated house I live in. She just sees me.

Chapter twenty-seven

Inbox:
Mia – call me, it's urgent.

I read the short, vague email from my boss. I'm not sure why, but I'm filled with anxiety as I reread the words, trying to quickly work out what could be so urgent.

I have met all my deadlines and I'm pretty sure my work is still up to a high standard, despite being a little distracted. I rack my brains, but the penny isn't dropping. I can't think of anything that would need to be met with such urgency.

I nervously dial the office number, holding my breath as the call tone plays into my ear.

"Mia?" My boss answers quicker than I expected. I'm surprised to hear an anxious tone in her voice. She's usually pretty confident and laid back.

"Yeah. Hi...what's happening? Is everything okay? Have I done everything okay?" I nervously question.

"Oh! Yes, yes of course. It's nothing to do with work."

"Oh?" I grow even more confused.

"It's Alex. I wasn't sure if I should tell you. I know you're divorced now, and you've moved on, but the news has spread pretty quickly, and I didn't want you to hear it through gossip."

I'm suddenly hit with so many mixed emotions. One small part of me is instantly annoyed that she is phoning me with this. This isn't my burden to take anymore. This isn't fair. But the rest of me is sick with nerves. The knot in my stomach is tight, I feel like I'm clenching every part of myself, but I can't stop it. My shoulders feel so heavy with stress.

"I... it's..." I realise I haven't managed a response and a long awkward pause has gone by. I do my best to speak but my throat feels dry. "Is he okay?"

"I don't know. It's been discussed in the office that Alex was found unconscious in his home after taking a lethal amount of alcohol and some prescription drugs."

Diazepam. It must be. He started relying on it a lot to relax when he felt himself getting panicky, or angry, or anything really. He used it to numb all his feelings. I suspected he was starting to abuse it, but I couldn't be sure at the time.

"Mia, are you still there?"

"I... I'll call him, maybe," I stutter. "Thank you for letting me know."

"That's really no problem. He's currently in St Andrew's Hospital. If we can do anything to help, please let us know," she kindly offers.

I feel a bit trembly when I hang up the phone which almost seems unfair to me. Alex shouldn't be my problem anymore and yet I still feel responsible.

Could he really have been trying to take his own life? Has our divorce tipped him too far? My god, if he died, would I be to blame? Was I a factor?

The questions are coming in too quickly and I can feel my chest growing tighter with each panicky thought.

Without thinking for another second, I grab my car keys from the kitchen counter and head out to take the two-hour journey to St Andrew's Hospital to see Alex. I have no idea if he wants to see me, or even whether I want to see him. But as much as I wish I didn't, I do feel responsible. And guilty. I can't just do nothing.

Usually when I get in my car, I sort out a playlist or faff around and find a good podcast about mysterious crimes or something to listen to and occupy my mind. But now I'm just driving in absolute silence. My mind is busy enough now without anything else. All I know is that I need to get there, I need to see if he can be okay on his own. If he can keep himself safe so this doesn't happen again. I need to know if I'm to blame, or if he needs me to help. It was one thing when he was self-medicating with alcohol and god knows what else, but I can't sit back and let him take his life.

I notice when I'm still twenty minutes away from the hospital that it's started to get dark. It's never appealed to me, driving in the dark, but I try not to worry about that right now.

"I'm sorry but we are only letting family into intensive care," the snooty receptionist informs me when I ask to see Alex.

"Intensive care?" I repeat. Even though I heard her perfectly the first time.

"Yes, intensive care. Are you a relative?"

"I'm, I'm...yes. I mean yes, I'm his wife," I lie. But I need to see him.

"Ah, I see. Okay, hang on. If you take a seat, I'll see if a nurse can take you round to where he is," she offers and points to a row of unappealing plastic green chairs in the corner.

I don't sit. I pace nervously instead. Walking between the door and back to the window, where I see through the darkness that it's now raining heavily. The rain beats down hard against the window, sporadically and almost deafening. I actually don't mind it though; it matches my sombre mood.

My stomach growls and it dawns on me that I haven't eaten a thing today, apart from my morning coffee.

There's a hot drinks machine in the corner of the room. I decide I'll have a cup of hot chocolate with an extra sugar to help keep my energy levels up whilst I wait. The hot liquid pours into my paper cup and gives me a small feeling of ease. There's something comforting about a hot drink. Which brings me back to the memory of my dad making me yummy hot chocolates with extra marshmallows when I was just a young girl.

The memory instantly brings a lump to my throat, and I do my best to pull myself together. I can't deal with any more emotions tonight. This hot chocolate is nothing like the ones my dad used to make. I take another sip but it's too watery for me, I can barely taste the sweetness of the chocolate.

"I can take you to see your husband now if you're ready," a friendly voice calls from the doorway.

I nod a little hesitantly before dropping my paper cup into the bin and following the nurse into the hallway.

"Thank you," I mutter and do my best to compose myself. I take a deep breath with an extra-long exhale. The nurse notices my anxiety because she looks at me sympathetically. Little does she know that I actually not long-ago divorced Alex. I'm most definitely not some hysterical wife who is worried sick and I'd hate for her to treat me like I am. I'm not sure I deserve any of her kindness.

"Okay, so, I'm not sure if you've been into an intensive care ward before but there will be lots of different beeps and occasionally the odd alarm. Your husband is attached to a fair few machines and wires. It can be really overwhelming but that's completely normal. If you have any questions for me at any time then please, just ask."

I nod politely but her sweet compassionate nature just makes me feel foolish. I'm starting to wonder if this was a massive mistake. I'm probably the last person he wants to see.

I try my best to avoid making eye contact with any of the other patients as we walk past numerous rooms. The further I walk down the hallway the more daunting this feels.

"Here she is! Your lovely wife has been waiting patiently to see you," the nurse cheerily says as I feel her hand gently on my back, guiding me into the room.

Alex is propped up in bed and staring right at me. There are a few wires and machines beeping but nowhere near as much as I was fearing. The nurse smiles at Alex before turning around and leaving the room.

"Wow. When they said my wife was here, I wasn't sure if I was still hallucinating," Alex jokes, his voice quite croaky but much more alert than I expected.

"Alex, what's going on?" I sigh loudly. "I had a call from work saying that you apparently took an overdose. I wasn't sure if I should come, but what's going on?"

I'm visibly fidgety and uncomfortable but Alex is calm and collected. He doesn't take his eyes off me as I pace his room, just like I was pacing the corridor moments ago.

"Well, let's see. My career is over, my bank account is running low, my family abandoned me and then my wife left me. Not exactly the life I thought I was going to have."

He says it calmly, but I can see the anger behind his eyes.

"What do you mean, your account is running low?" I ask, avoiding the part about me. He picks up on it too because he smirks and rolls his eyes.

"Well, my career is over. You were there when it happened, remember?"

"I know, but you were a huge deal at one point. What happened to doing television appearances and sports commentating? I thought you said those were your plans?"

"Strangely Mia, nobody wants to hire you when word gets around that your wife left you because you drink too much and throw your weight around."

"I didn't tell anyone anything! I promise," I blurt out quickly to avoid an argument.

"I know but come on, it doesn't take long for people to find out these things does it? It was always going to happen."

I nod in agreement and take a seat next to his bed.

"Alex...what happened to your funds?" I press, gently.

"Cocaine, prostitutes, gambling." He answers so coldly it makes me shiver.

"Why, Alex? Why?" I shake my head, trying to make sense of the mess that has been occurring since I left.

"You couldn't understand. You couldn't possibly. And what you did understand you didn't like, which is why you left. So why are you here now? I'm still the same wreck you left behind."

"I thought maybe you would have been on your feet by now. I thought you would have moved on. Become happier." I shrug, guiltily.

"Like you then?" he fires back.

"I'm...still single."

"Where do you live?"

"In the countryside."

"Ah I see." He scoffs. "Nice place, the countryside. Heard it has some lovely pubs."

"It's not like that. It's not a secret where I live. I just like being off the radar a little bit."

"Can I come there?" he asks, his eyes pleading with mine.

"To my house?"

"Yes. Please. Just for a few days," he confirms.

"But...why? Why my house?" I ask, taken aback.

"I set mine on fire," he answers and looks nervously down at his slightly sweaty palms. "I took an overdose and then I set a fire and waited to die from the drugs or to be burnt with my house. Whatever came first."

"Oh, Alex," I sigh. It hurts to hear what he has been going through. We may be divorced but I did love him once. This is the last thing I would have ever wanted for him.

"My agent...well, he isn't my agent anymore because I can't afford him. But as a friend, he is sorting me out a rental. He says he is going to help get me on my feet, but I need a place to crash for a little while and he doesn't have the space. But it's fine, I don't expect your help. I didn't even expect to see you again. Even now. I'll find a hotel or something."

"No Alex, it's fine. I came here because I was worried and because I wanted to do something. If this helps you, I can do it. You can stay with me for a little while, we'll make it work." I smile.

"Really?" he croaks, looking relieved. I nod and give him a reassuring smile.

"Thank you," he simply says, gratefully.

"When do you think you'll be well enough to leave?"

"Well, they are trying to find me a space on the ward for tomorrow. I've already been here for a few days now and they said my levels are better. So, I think maybe two- or three-days' time. Is that going to work for you?"

"Sure. Don't worry about anything else for now. Like I said, we'll make it work until you're back on your feet."

I stay for another hour or so. I get the feeling that he hasn't had many visitors, and this is the first chance he has had to really talk to someone.

The drive home is a bit of a daze. Mentally, I'm exhausted. I never thought I'd see Alex again once our divorce papers came through. I knew he was still struggling with a lot of his demons when I left but I had no idea just how bad things would get for him.

Tomorrow, I'm supposed to be spending the weekend with Jacob. I should be at home getting ready to finally spend some real time with the man who has taken over my thoughts on a daily basis. But instead I'm working out how to break the news to him that I have just invited my ex-husband to come and stay in my home with me.

I'm a little worried about his reaction, given how angry he was when he caught me with that farmer guy I met at the bar. I'm hoping he can understand this though. I can't just turn my back on Alex when he is in this state. What sort of person would I be if I did?

Alex's dejected face keeps popping into my mind during the

long drive home which keeps overwhelming me with guilt and sadness.

Every time I question whether I am doing the right thing I see his face. My friends will probably think I am absolutely insane for getting involved with him again, even if it is just as a friend, but I'd like to think that if the tables were turned, he would help me too.

Or maybe I'm easing my own guilt by offering myself as a Florence Nightingale. Either way, I'm committed now and I'm going to help him until he is ready to move into his new place, which hopefully won't be too long anyway.

By the time I pull into my driveway, the street is silent. The few houses on the block are in darkness, Jacob's too; only a glowing streetlamp offers me enough light to get from my car to my front door safely.

Should I be worried that you're only just getting home? -J

The message flashes up on my screen and instantly makes me smile. I can't get into where I have been, not this late and certainly not over text. So, my reply is simple:

Are you stalking me?

With an added wink emoji for good measure.

I grab a bottle of water out of the fridge and head straight up to my bed. I kick my shoes off and flop down onto my bouncy mattress.

I notice another message on my screen, just before I give in and allow my heavy eyelids to close:

Sweet dreams -J

Chapter twenty-eight

I'm not usually a light sleeper but I'm awoken in what feels like the middle of the night by a car door slamming just outside my window. I tap my phone screen to see that it's almost five in the morning; it must be Elle leaving for the airport.

I tiptoe carefully across the room and peer out of the window just in time to see the taxi driver close the door behind her and drive away.

Watching her taxi disappear into the night and knowing that Jacob is free to be with me for the entire weekend only makes me happy for a split second before the guilt washes over me.

Elle has no idea what she's driving away from. She thinks she's just going on a girlie weekend and she's probably very excited, but she has no clue of what's about to happen. She has no idea that her husband has invited me to spend the weekend with him and that I've accepted. She has no idea that it's all I have been thinking about these last couple of days. Whilst she was packing her bags, I was waxing my legs and sprucing myself up because I wanted to be as beautiful as I could be for the man that *she* is married to.

Is this really the person you want to be Mia?

Here we go, the thickness is back to taking over my throat and my eyes are spilling with tears. I hate it when I go back and forth about Jacob, because I know in my heart that I genuinely feel something for him. Something that I didn't have before, but it's not mine.

Images of Alex laid up in his hospital bed now take over my mind and I start to feel like I may be the problem here. The evidence would suggest that I'm leaving a trail of destruction wherever I go and now it looks as though I'm starting to do it all over again.

My divorce from Alex pushed him over the edge and he couldn't cope anymore. And now I'm somebody's affair. I'm the reason why Elle's heart will break. I'll be the reason why people will hate me for coming between them. I'll be the reason why Jacob will no doubt have a huge ugly divorce battle on his hands. I'll be the reason why his family will be hugely disappointed that he ran off with some sportswriter with no status or well-known family. And above all else, I'm becoming the reason why I hate myself.

The messes of my life become crystal clear. Everything around me is so difficult and it's all my fault.

I don't want to lose Jacob, but I don't want to be in love like this.

I have the idea to do something that I haven't done in probably ten years or so. I pull out a spare journal from the box under my bed and I let everything that's whirling around my head spill out onto the paper instead.

I write about how much I miss my dad. I write about Alex and how I desperately want him to bounce back and find some real happiness. I write about how much I wish I was in whichever exotic country my mum is currently in because this life I have created is scaring me. I would run from it if I could.

One minute I was fantasising about talking to Jacob until the sun comes up and now, I'm ready to walk away from everything. I'm not sure if it's seeing Alex so broken or watching Elle drive away so oblivious to what's happening, but something in me has suddenly connected and now I can see it all so clearly.

But walking away from Jacob won't be easy. I know it won't. The second I'm in the same room as him I lose all control. I get so consumed by him. By the way he talks to me, the way he dresses, especially the way his white t-shirts cling to him. I get lost tracing the tattoos on his arms. And each time he looks into my eyes, I know all my feelings are only getting stronger. Everything about him consumes me.

Today I know exactly what I must do, and I'm determined to do it and change everything for the better. It's a relief to see that the skies are slowly getting lighter. It won't be long before I can get out of the house and make a start.

On a fresh page of my journal, I start making notes of the things I need to do. I scribble down a little list of things I'll need to get to accommodate Alex for a few days, including an extra duvet set; he can take my bed and I'll sleep on the sofa. I'll also pick up a few essentials for him like aftershave and a toothbrush and all the necessities he probably hasn't got with him.

I add some notes for the supermarket. I'll try and get Alex some of his favourite foods, hopefully it will bring him some comfort. I don't want to write it down, but I make a mental note to hide any bottles of wine or vodka that I have left around the house. It's important he stays sober and I need to do everything I can to support that.

Reluctantly, I make my last note and I fight back the tears as my pen touches the paper. I note down the phone number for the estate agents. Today I'm going to put my beautiful forever home back onto the market. I have no choice. I can't live here and be certain that I'll never cross the line with Jacob again and I definitely can't watch him be with Elle for the rest of our lives. I just can't. My heart feels broken enough without adding salt to the wound. I need a clean break, we both do.

Even if I don't fully see it now, I will one day. And I'm sure he will too, hopefully. I'll thank myself for being as strong as I'm being right now.

My head feels clearer already just by writing everything down and making my plan. I lie back on my bed and plug in my headphones; music has always been a comfort when I need it the most.

When I hit play, the first song on my list is *Skinny Love* by Birdie. It's a slow tempo song with lyrics that I can get lost in. I almost skip it to avoid growing more emotional, but instead I decide that it's okay to embrace the pain. It's okay to grieve for what could have been.

I close my eyes to escape but all I see is him. I squeeze my pillow tight as the words play gently.

Who will love you?
Who will fight?
Who will fall far behind?

Chapter twenty-nine: Jacob's point of view

It's taken me all day to get everything that I wanted to get for Mia prepared. I had to go shopping in places I've never been before, into little quirky trinket shops and pretty much anywhere with home written on the sign. It took me hours, but I wanted to get as close to the real deal as I possibly could.

Mia opened up to me about her close relationship with her dad and how thoughtfully he would comfort her and cheer her up when she really needed it and how it would always start with a mug of hot chocolate. Her dad would make it on the hob with Cornish milk and then pour it into an extra-large red teapot so that Mia could refill as much as she wanted. Then he'd put out a wooden tray filled with marshmallows, cream, sprinkles and chocolate buttons that she got to decorate her drink with.

I have no idea what makes a hot drink so magic, but I do know it made Mia feel so safe. And she misses it desperately. When she mentions her dad, I can see the ache behind her eyes and the shift in her demeanour. I want to try, somehow, to recreate the warmth he gave her. I want her to feel safe.

My palms are sweating as I arrange everything on the kitchen counter. I have never done anything like this before. I have never wanted to do anything like this either. Elle always wanted the same thing: she wanted to be whisked to the most expensive restaurant I could find, presented with a new piece of jewellery from Tiffany or Cartier and she wanted to take at least five photos during our evening to share on her social media.

Whereas Mia is more intricate. Sure, she'd be grateful for any gift I could offer her, but when she speaks about her life, her face lights up at the memories and the moments and not at all the materialistic stuff we're influenced to buy. I think that's my favourite thing of all. I love the way she sees the world and her place in it, and when I'm with her, I feel like I have that vision too.

These thoughts have me buckled under the realisation of how quickly these feelings came for her. I've never felt this way and honestly, I didn't expect to. She went from being the hot girl next door that I occasionally fantasised about fucking to the one thing I need the most to get me through the day. All I think about is the day I can get out of this web of lies and be with her openly and happily. I now fantasise more about all the places I want to take her, all the moments I want to experience with her just so I can make her smile. I want to live my life the way I should always have. With the right person.

If I have to give up everything for this then I will. If Elle wants the house, half my money, all my cars, then fuck it, she can have it. As long as she signs those papers and allows this escapade to finally end, I'll do whatever she wants. I'll take all the blame. I'll tell the family that it was my fault, that I couldn't be the man she needed or wanted in life. I'll move out, I won't let this disrupt her life. I'll move hours away from here if I have to, if it makes her happy enough to let me go without a fight.

But as these thoughts come, I have a horrible feeling in the pit of my stomach. I think a fight is exactly what I will have. It's not me she won't want to lose as such, it's this lifestyle. That and the fact that divorce is practically a swear word for her people. Divorce equals failure for her and I know she'll struggle to see it any other way.

**

A subtle knock sounds against my front door; I barely hear it over the heavy rain that's been battering against my windows for the last hour. She's earlier than expected but I don't care, I'm ready for her. I'm ready to spend the next few days enjoying her.

I rush across the entrance hall ready for her to fall into me and wrap her arms tightly around me. But that hope fades the second I lay my eyes on her.

"Mia?" I ask, concerned.

Her eyes are puffy, she looks like she's been crying for hours; her arms are folded against her chest and her head is slightly dropped down as if she's ready to defend herself or apologise for something. I'm not sure which but either way I have a bad feeling. Her soft blonde hair is dripping wet and her mascara has smudged around her perfectly green eyes.

"Can we talk?" she finally croaks, her voice sounding strained and exhausted.

"You're soaked...what's going on?" I grab hold of her arm and gently guide her towards me so I can wrap my arms around her to keep her warm. She doesn't embrace me like I thought she would, but she hasn't pushed me away either.

"I'm fine. I just went for a little walk before I came over. I just needed a minute to myself that's all."

I want to ask her why the hell she went walking in this weather, but I decide it's best not to.

She takes a step back and wipes the rain from her face and pushes her hair back anxiously as I grab a towel from the downstairs cupboard and throw it around her shoulders.

"O-kay?" I gently question, confused.

Mia leads the way into the kitchen, and I follow behind, my body suddenly filled with uncertainty and dread. She barely made eye contact with me at the door and she's shivering a little. At first, I thought she was cold from the rain but as I look at her closely, I think it's nerves. Which scares the hell out of me?

Suddenly, a gasp falls from her lips; she's stopped dead in her tracks and is just staring motionless at the counter.

"What's this?" she whispers as her bottom lip quivers and her eyes effortlessly fill with tears.

"Well...it was supposed to be a surprise. Something to make you smile," I answer honestly as her eyes peer over at the special mug I got her and the red teapot, just like the one she described from her past.

"How?" she mumbled just before a tear fell from her cheek.

"I went exploring this morning, down to those little shops across town and just kept looking until I found all the things just like you described."

She gulps hard and I'm struggling to read her right now.

"Why?" her scratchy voice manages to ask me.

"I just remembered you telling me about those special moments your dad created for you. When you needed it most? I don't know, I figured it would show you how much you mean to me." I scramble to explain myself, but she doesn't look up from the counter. Tears continue to fall and I'm panicking that I've messed all this up already.

"Mia, please talk to me. Say something. Have I fucked up? I'm sorry...this was supposed to make you happy..."

Please baby, just talk to me.

Chapter thirty

My chest is rising quickly up and down as I fight to hold back my emotions and try my very best to stay in control.

It's the most thoughtful thing I have ever seen in my life. I can't stop staring because I don't ever want to forget this moment. I want this picture in my mind forever. This is without a doubt the most amazing thing anyone has ever done for me, to bring me back a piece of my dad.

"You've recreated a moment from my past," I say before the emotions get the better of me and I break down with harder breaths and more tears.

For the first time since I arrived, I allow myself to gaze up and look into Jacob's eyes. He looks terrified, like he is the cause of this pain, but he isn't. It's just so beautiful that I can't think straight.

"Because those memories are important to you. So, I wanted you to know that they're important to me too. Everything about you is important to me," he answers, rushed and panicked.

This is now a million times harder. I came here to tell him it's over and that I'm going to be leaving and now I walk into the most romantic and thoughtful gesture that is so beyond anything I could have ever thought up. It's left me completely winded.

The idea of never seeing him again terrifies me and I find myself visibly shaking my head at the mess I find myself in.

"Shit. I'm so sorry. I'll pack it all away now, I'll bin it if you want. It was a stupid fucking idea and I'm so sorry..." Jacob blurts, obviously taking me shaking my head as some sort of answer.

"No, don't!" I cry. "I love it so much, I really do."

"I don't understand?" Jacob's face screws up and I can tell he is starting to feel stressed. He pushes his hands through his hair anxiously and takes a few steps away from me and paces the kitchen.

"What's going on?"

"I can't..." I start to say before stopping myself. Jacob turns around, frustrated, and puts his arms against the wall as he leans against it. I can see he is losing his patience.

This is all so much to bear right now, I wasn't expecting this. I can't process it all, it's all too much. I feel like the room is whirling around me but really, it's probably just my thoughts racing. It's just as scary though. I can't seem to slow them down and before I know it, I'm so overwhelmed I can't think straight anymore.

"I have to go!" I shout before rushing to the door.

I feel a split second of relief when I open the front door and the air hits my face, but it's quickly taken away when the door suddenly slams back shut and Jacob spins me round by the arm to face him.

"Mia, you can't leave me like this. It'll drive me wild," he breathes as he gazes intently down at me.

My throat feels so thick from trying to desperately conceal my pain. Jacob's eyes narrow as he continues to hold his gaze onto mine. My heart is thumping so hard I can feel it in my neck.

My mouth is so dry, but I try to force the words out.

"Jacob...I..."

"Having a panic attack?" he answers for me and I nod tearfully.

He drops his head down so that it gently leans against mine and he carefully grips my trembly hand into his before bringing it up to his chest.

"Feel how I'm breathing, Mia. Concentrate. Follow my rhythm," he gently soothes as he uses his other hand to tuck a little bit of hair behind my ear.

"Slow it down for me baby. Breathe in through your nose, slowly, hold it for a second and breathe out through your mouth."

I follow his instructions and I'm relieved when it seems to be working. I'm not sure whether it's following his breathing or the way he is towering over me, holding me close against his body, but I suddenly feel safe and calm enough to control my breathing again.

"Thank you," I whisper gratefully, keeping my hand against his chest.

"Mia, I don't know what's going on, and I know we said we would wait. But I'm done waiting," he breathes as he brings his hand up to cup my cheek.

Gently he traces my bottom lip with his thumb. I open my mouth to speak but nothing comes out. Instead, I'm met with the warmth of his soft lips pushed against mine. Everything I have needed to say to him has become a blur. I can't concentrate on anything other than this moment of being held beneath him. I welcome the feel of his tongue as it glides over mine and I let myself drown in this moment between us. I allow my hand to leave his chest and slowly slide up to the back of his head where

I gently caress the nape of his neck.

"I'm going to take you to my room now," he says into my mouth, authoritatively.

He immediately slides both hands down underneath my bum before picking me up and pulling me up to his waist. I instantly follow his lead by wrapping my legs tightly around him as he carries me away into his man cave.

Jacob lays me down gently onto his couch and pulls his white t-shirt up and over his head before dropping it down onto the floor next to us. His hands gently tug at my top and I lean up momentarily, just enough for him to guide it up and off my body. I lie back, feeling his warm frame completely engulfing my petite body.

My busy mind has finally settled and all I can think about is how much this feels right. I belong here.

I tilt my head up to lock in the gaze from his big brown eyes. We blink slowly in unison as we soak in each other's raw authentic selves.

I take my hands down from his shoulders and allow them to find the buckle of his belt. I pull it open and my fingers carefully unbutton his jeans before sliding down the zip. His hands meet mine and together we push down his jeans and his white boxer briefs before he is left completely naked.

In return, I start unbuttoning my trousers and his eyes light up as I begin pulling them down. His swollen lips begin kissing along my hip bone as he takes over the undressing and carefully slides them down my legs.

I welcome the weight of him against my body as he drops back down onto me and closes the gap between our lips. The way our lips glide over each other is so intoxicating that a soft moan leaves my mouth. I think it makes him even more excited because I can feel his pounding heartbeat against my own chest.

He hungrily kisses my neck before sliding down and sucking at my breasts. Intense moans erupt from his mouth and I feel more turned on than I ever have in my life. I can feel the heat growing between my legs and just at that moment, Jacob reaches down and runs his fingers over the front of my thong, feeling my wetness.

"Fuck," Jacob pants as he pushes my legs further apart.

He continues to rub gently over my most swollen area and I find myself biting hard on my lip to stop myself screaming his name.

"Take them off..." I plead as I arch my back and he does as I ask.

I reach down and feel his hard erection against the palm of my hand which quickens his breathing. I line him up with my throbbing entrance and his eyes widen in excitement.

"There'll be no going back after this Mia. You know that, right?" and I nod helplessly underneath his broad sweaty body.

"I don't want to go back. Not now," I say through panting breaths.

"Tell me that it'll only be me and you from now on?" Jacob breathes with a demanding tone in his voice. I barely have a second to answer before I feel every inch of him push deeply inside of me.

I gasp hard and arch my back. Pushing myself harder onto him.

"It's going to be me and you, Jacob," I whimper as I melt into him.

His hands slide up to meet mine, pinning my wrists on each side of my head and he begins to thrust feverishly in and out of me.

"Fuck, Mia," he groans, struggling to keep himself under control and I love knowing that he is as vulnerable as I am.

Jacob carefully releases my wrists and instead his fingers entwine with mine; his pace has slowed a little, becoming gentler again as he kisses me passionately. Savouring every moment.

The steady rhythm causes my breasts to gently bounce up and down, his lips graze them with every movement.

I can feel myself growing close with each thrust. I know Jacob is getting close too, but I don't want this to end.

"Wrap your legs around me, Mia," Jacob mumbles against my red pouted lips. I oblige quickly just as his thrusts become harder again.

"I'm so close," I moan and throw my head back as I feel the pressure mounting between my legs.

My fingers push through his thick brown hair and I grip it hard as I feel myself ready to climax.

His thrusts speed up as my back arches harder into him, forcing him even deeper inside me.

A mixture of our pleasurable moans fills the room as an orgasm takes over my body and Jacob buries his head into my breasts as I feel his warmth explode inside of me. Our breathing becomes synchronised as our bodies slowly relax into each other.

I see a glisten of sweat across his shoulder blade before he picks his head back up to look into my eyes.

I bask in the moment of our heated bodies pressed together. Jacob's eyes study me carefully, they gaze up over the curve of my breasts, onto my collarbone before eventually coming back and locking into my eyes.

"I love you, Mia," he softly whispers.

Chapter thirty-one

I'm awoken early by the sound of a lawnmower nearby. Jacob's hand is still draped across my stomach and his face is nestled against my arm, the same way he fell asleep last night. I realise now just how early we did fall asleep – we didn't even wake again for dinner. I'm not surprised though on my part – the crying, the panic attack and then the sex completely wiped me out. So many emotions in such a short space of time. I definitely needed a good sleep. Especially after being up most of the night before.

My stomach growls underneath the weight of him and I'm definitely ready for some food. I can't remember the last time I ate.

Before I contemplate getting up, flashbacks from last night start to flood my thoughts and the most exciting one of course is the moment Jacob said he loved me. The way he studied every inch of my naked body. I felt so vulnerable underneath him, in a way that made me all his and he felt like all mine.

A soft groan falls from Jacob's plump lips as he stretches and carefully opens his eyes. Immediately his eyes lock with mine and a smile spreads across his face.

"Morning," he whispers in a sleepy husky voice.

He looks perfect, even with his hair slightly dishevelled – if anything, it makes him even sexier.

"Morning," I reply with a smile and playfully tug at his messy hair.

"Stop it, you'll get me horny," he says as he jokingly swats my hand away.

I giggle loudly at the ridiculous comment. I probably look like something from a zombie movie right now. My eyes still feel puffy and my make-up is probably smudged all over the place.

"Sure!" I sarcastically jeer.

Jacob takes hold of my hand, which was resting on my stomach, and pulls it down to feel his hard length.

"See?" he says with a smirk.

I roll my eyes and giggle at his playfulness.

As he looks back up, his expression becomes more serious. But still gentle.

"There are some things I want to talk to you about, but first I thought you could jump in the shower and get ready, because there's somewhere special I want to take you," he continues softly before tucking a bit of hair behind my ear and stroking my cheek with his thumb.

Immediately his touch gives me goosebumps all over my skin and my heart speeds up slightly. I nod in agreement and lean down to give him a gentle kiss before I head off to the bathroom. He holds me against his lips for a few seconds longer with his hand now firmly around the back of my neck.

I could quite easily lie here with him all day but I'm eager to see this special place. I love surprises.

I head back to mine for a change of clothes; the weather still isn't great, so I opt for some dark blue jeans, ankle boots and a long brown jacket over a cream turtleneck jumper. I give my face a good wash too after my shower and finish by reapplying some subtle make-up. Nothing over the top but just enough to give me some colour back in my cheeks and some volume to my lashes.

Before I know it, I see Jacob already heading for his black car. I quickly try to silence my hungry stomach by eating a banana before grabbing a bottle of water and heading out to meet him.

He looks unbelievably handsome. As the weather is starting to change, so is his fashion. I love the way these new jumpers cling to him – although he is more covered, you can still make out his thick arm muscles through the fabric. He looks casual, but sexy.

"Wow," he breathes as I climb into the seat next to him. "You look beautiful, Mia. Beautiful."

My cheeks blush red at his romantic compliment. They are something I'm not really used to. In fact, most compliments make me feel awkward. Alex once said he thought I looked extremely sexy in some red heels I wore one Christmas and I replied by asking him if he'd like to borrow them. I remember the way his eyebrow arched, and he looked at me as if I was crazy before we both erupted with laughter.

It's different when Jacob compliments me though. It's like he is informing me of some important fact that I need to know. It's not like just his observation, it's something everybody thinks about me. It makes me feel so desirable, the most wanted I have ever been, and that in turn makes me feel sexy and confident. It makes me want Jacob even more. Every single time.

"So where are we going?" I ask, changing the topic from me so my burning cheeks can cool down at least.

"You'll see. But it's about twenty minutes away. Here, put some music on," Jacob says, as he hands me his phone with his playlist on display.

I see a lot of American rappers, some names I'm familiar with such as Eminem, Drake and Nas, but quite a few I have never heard of.

My thumb scrolls through the many songs but I'm unsure of what to put on. I decide to just stick anything on as I'm taking so long, and I hit shuffle.

"Good choice," Jacob smiles as the loud beat fills the car.

...She say I'm obsessed with thick women and I agree, yeha
That's right I like my girls BBW, yeah
Type that wanna suck you dry and then eat some lunch with you, yeah
So thick that everyone else in the room is so uncomfortable...

"Um..." I mutter, shocked, as Jacob begins to laugh at me.

"Have you not got any, I don't know, any..."

"Little Mix?" He sarcastically interrupts me with a big smile across his face, showing off his perfectly white teeth.

"No, actually! I wasn't going to say that. Although, I mean, they are a great band, if we're being honest!" I say, making Jacob laugh even more.

"What were you going to say then?"

"I don't know, just music that's more fun. Like eighties?"

"I LOVE the eighties!" Jacob beams. "Come out of that and you'll see a whole eighties playlist below it."

"Oh my god, I literally love the eighties too!" I join in, excitedly.

"Of course, you do." He winks.

I do my best to ignore his teasing and search through the other playlist. Instantly my face lights up as I see more songs I recognise and love.

"OH MY GOD!" I blurt excitedly. "Technically, this is a seventies song, but I'll take it. Ready? We gotta sing this together."

"No way!" Jacob protests, shaking his head dramatically. "We are not about to get cheesy!"

"Oh, Jacob. We are SO about to get cheesy!"

I click on the song and instantly Elton John and Kiki Dee blare into the speakers and I proudly stare at Jacob who looks mortified.

"Okay, I'll start. I'll sing Elton's part and you can be Kiki."

"Fuck off!" he blurts as if I'm crazy but still maintains his gorgeous bright smile.

"Here we go! Let's do this. Don't go breaking my heart…" I bellow at the top of my voice, only to be met with silence.

I pause the song and start it again.

"I've got all day Jacob," I shrug carelessly.

"You're such a cheese ball!" He laughs at my teasing.

"Don't go breaking my heart…" I sing again.

"I couldn't if I tried." Jacob joins in with almost a hundred percent effort which completely takes me by surprise and I nearly snort from laughing so hard.

"Oh, honey if I get restless…"

"Baby, you're not that kind…" Jacob follows on.

We both fall about laughing as we continue to bellow the song in turns. Randomly, Jacob takes hold of my hand and brings it to his chest whilst keeping the other on the steering wheel.

"I love you, you bloody cheese ball." He smiles, causing butterflies to fill my belly.

"I love you too, Kiki." I smile back.

Chapter thirty-two

I'm almost disappointed when I notice that we are starting to pull over and that our car journey full of cheesy karaoke songs has come to an end.

"It's a muddy field?" I ask, confused.

"It's what is on the other side of the muddy field that counts," he reassures me before getting out and opening my car door for me, like the gentleman he is.

I feel so excited about our little adventure out that I don't even mind one bit that my boots are getting covered in mud already.

As we walk deeper into the field, our surroundings grow quieter and I can see nothing but green grass, that is until we come to a small footpath through some woods.

"Do you have a favourite movie, Mia?" Jacob asks and watches attentively for my answer.

"Hmm, that's a tough one really. It depends what I'm in the mood for. Although I am a true sucker for a romantic comedy. Why do you ask?"

"Well, it kind of ties in with where we're going. When I was a kid my favourite movie was *My Girl*. Have you seen it?"

"Of course! 'Wanna go tree climbing Thomas J?'" I giggle as I quote the movie.

"It's a classic."

"It is, but I didn't think it was a movie boys would have enjoyed that much?"

Jacob puts his hands in his jacket pockets and shifts a little awkwardly as his face looks busy trying to find the right words.

"I think I loved it because it was just so different. My family were all highly educated professionals with a very organised lifestyle. Every bit of their life was planned and mapped out, just like mine was. Before I even had a say," he begins to explain.

I nod along as I listen carefully. I can tell by his soft voice that what he is saying is important to him. I get the feeling this is a side he doesn't expose often.

"Well, in the film, Vada's dad was like some funeral director, and I remember thinking it was so random and different. Then he met Shelley who was hugely free spirited. She even rocked up in a trailer. Then there was Vada herself who was so unconventional. She spent all of her time outside, exploring and having fun. Living just the way she wanted to. She didn't fit in with the girl group but that didn't matter, because she had Thomas J. Do you know what I'm trying to say? Or am I just completely fucking this up?" He sighs as he stops in his tracks and turns to face me.

"I think you're trying to tell me that you wish your life was more unpredictable?"

"Yes. I wanted a real childhood. I wanted to explore the outdoors, climb trees and ride a bike. I wanted to be left alone to discover what it is that I'm passionate about. Vada ended up finding out that she loved poetry – my god, my parents scoffed at that part of the movie. I so desperately wanted my life to be free like that though. But more than anything else, I wanted my Vada," he says as his thumb gently brushes over my lips.

"Now who's the cheese ball?" I smirk just as he pushes his lips against mine and I bring my arms up to wrap tightly around his neck as his warm tongue slides over mine.

After he pulls away, he takes me by the hand and leads me out the other side of the woods and onto a bank, revealing a breathtakingly beautiful lake in front of me. It's huge. You'd think it would be such a popular spot for visitors but it's so quiet. I can hear nothing but the birds in the trees.

In front of us is a long wooden fishing platform. Instantly it makes me think of something very familiar.

"It reminds me of the scene in the film, where Vada and Thomas J became blood brothers," he answers, as if he just read my mind. "And I love it. It's one of my favourite places I have ever had the luck of finding and up until now I have never told another soul about it. Not even Elle."

"It's stunning. A real place to get some head space from the world," I say, taking in the view around me.

I catch Jacob intently enjoying my positive reaction to his secret place.

"It's where I have been coming to figure everything out. I've been talking to my solicitor and we've decided it's best I move out of the house as soon as I have told Elle. I don't want her to think I'm trying to take everything away from her. I don't want her to react any worse than I already expect her to. I have rented a house near here."

"Wow," is all I manage to say. I knew we were obviously getting to this point. It needed to happen. But hearing the words surprises me still.

"I'll give her a day or two when she's back from Cape Verde to get over all the partying she'll have been doing and then I'll sit her down and tell her," he continues as he takes a few steps towards me, closing the gap between us.

Holy shit. It's all getting so real. I want Jacob more than anything, but I'd be lying to myself if I said I wasn't scared. I'm scared of hurting people; I'm scared of getting hurt and mostly I'm scared of Jacob's entire life turning upside down.

"But you love your house?" I say, anxiety thick in my voice.

"No, I don't! When did I say that? I love my man cave, there's a difference." Jacob chuckles. "Besides, if I have to lose it all to start a new life with you, then so be it."

"Are you sure about this?"

"Mia. You're everything I didn't even know I needed until I met you. You've opened my eyes to so much. I've learned about the kind of man I am and the kind of man I want to be. Before you, my life was afternoon teas at the Ritz, shopping in Covent Garden and glitzy house parties with people I can't even stand. All because I was trying to impress even more people I can't stand. Then I met a crazy girl who lights up at the mention of sports, gets drunk and becomes best friends with a stray cat, swears at her vacuum and gets naked in my hot tub. You are crazy in a wonderful way. Because of you, I've become crazy. I'm sneaking around like a teenager in love. Something I never thought in a million years I could be capable of, it's way more drama than I would ever want to entertain. But I just can't keep away from you, no matter how hard I tried at the start, you're like a magnet to me. I feel the best I have ever felt when I'm with you. I can't lose that."

My eyes sting as my overwhelming emotions spill over the surface. I swallow hard to try and conceal my feelings, although it's clear Jacob can see the small tear leaving the corner of my eye. I wipe it quickly away before smiling up at his big brown eyes.

"A simple yes would have done," I sarcastically tease and playfully nudge him.

He simply rolls his eyes with a big grin before dropping his forehead down slightly, so it rests gently against mine.

"I don't have all the answers. I'm not sure what house we will end up living in, or even if it'll still be around here. I can't promise that this won't get messy, but I can promise that I'm going to protect you as best I can. I just need you to promise me that you'll be mine," he says so softly that it's almost a whisper.

I nod instantly against his forehead without even thinking. It's the easiest question I have ever had to answer. As I tilt my head up towards him, I catch a look of relief in his eyes. He has needed to have this reassurance for a while now, I can tell. I truly can't believe what is about to happen.

But for him, I'm ready.

Chapter thirty-three

By the time we get home, the temperature has dropped below freezing and every breath I take from the car to Jacob's house is misted up in front of me.

Winter is definitely on its way. I have been so distracted lately that I barely noticed that the colours of the trees were all changing and most of the leaves were on the floor already.

Suddenly, Jacob takes me by the hand and pulls me along quickly as heavy raindrops begin to fall around me.

"Shit!" I scream as I giggle and pick up the pace to keep up with him.

We make it inside just as the rain beats down heavily on the ground, instantly creating large puddles and soaking everything within seconds. The angry clouds gather above us, suggesting we are in for some kind of storm.

"I guess we made it back just in time." Jacob smiles as he uses his hand to shake off the raindrops from his thick dark hair.

I admire the chaos of his hair as it flops over to one side. Usually it is perfectly styled to match his professional demeanour, but this relaxed look is definitely my favourite.

Jacob pulls his sweater up over his head, momentarily revealing his warm chiselled body and of course my wandering eyes are immediately fixated on him. I stare hungrily at the slight indents beside his hip bones and remember how the weight of his body felt on top of mine. I can't help but picture myself tugging at his messy hair right now and visualising him taking over my body and filling me with pleasure.

"Stop it." Jacob startles me.

"W-what?"

"Staring at me like that. It's like you're undressing me with your eyes, and it'll turn me on." He sighs, as if he is trying to tell me off but his smirk gives him away.

"No idea what you're talking about. Seriously. Don't flatter yourself," I say with a shrug and nonchalantly walk away towards the kitchen.

"Oh okay, we're playing that game, are we?" he says before chasing me into the next room and playfully wrestling me.

Giggling, I wriggle free from his clutches and run around the kitchen island to grab the spray cream from the fridge.

"Don't you dare!" Jacob half authoritatively shouts. "That's for the hot chocolates I got you for later. And... maybe one or two other things as the night goes on."

"Oh really?!" I jeer sarcastically which forces Jacob to laugh before he chases me round the island.

As Jacob grabs hold of me, we fall to the kitchen floor, laughing. I land on his lap and he embraces me by pulling me closer and guiding my legs until they're wrapped around his waist.

I can't help but wonder whether he has ever had moments like this with Elle. Although I struggle to see it. I can't imagine Elle risking a crease in her two hundred-pound jeans, or sitting on a floor for that matter, and I think that's what makes this all the better. This side of Jacob is new. It's new for him. I don't think he has ever been this raw and honest with anyone before. This is the real Jacob. Behind the money and the expensive suits. This is him.

"Has anyone else ever got to see you smile like this?" I blurt out, completely engulfed in this moment.

Jacob looks up at my face and studies me carefully. He has a mixture of uncertainty and worry in his eyes, like he has had some flicker of realisation and vulnerability, but finally, he swallows hard to compose his emotions and shakes his head to answer me, before grasping the back of my neck with his hand and pulling me in close for a kiss.

His lips come at mine faster than before, like he is hungry to taste me. The passion takes me by surprise, but I welcome it as I groan gently against his full lips. Instantly, he responds to it with urgency. Before I know it, I'm laid back on the kitchen floor, tugging his t-shirt over his head and panting at the very thought of what's about to happen.

"I need you," I whimper through my heavy panting.

My jeans are off within seconds as Jacob lowers his boxers, revealing his hard length ready for me. I can feel my cheeks burning already, my throat feels dry, my skin sensitive to the touch and I'm absolutely throbbing in between my legs.

Just as Jacob towers over me he stops for a split second and smiles. Instead of entering me, his head drops down and he lowers his mouth towards my most sensitive part. I bite down on my bottom lip as I await in anticipation for his touch.

He sloppily kisses my inner thighs so intensely it makes my back arch. I love the warm wetness spilling from his mouth onto my skin.

He roughly spreads my legs wider apart and gives me one last glance before burying his head into me, gently stroking his warm tongue against my folds before gliding up against my swollen bud.

"Oh fuck," I gasp dramatically as my fingers find their way into his hair. I tug hard with every lick and suck of my most sensitive area. Heat radiates from my body the closer I get to climaxing.

Without warning his manly fingers suddenly enter me, pushing deeply in and out between licks.

I can feel beads of sweat against my neck as the adrenaline pumps through me.

Jacob's hands grip tightly onto my hips as he encourages me to rock them slightly against his mouth. I instantly follow his instructions which heightens the intensity.

"I'm close," I murmur.

Jacob's eyes darken as he watches me joyously. He shoots me an arrogant smile, almost as if he knows he is the best I have ever had, before returning to pleasure me.

With one last flick of his tongue, he takes me to the edge, and I can no longer hold myself back. My legs quiver beneath him as I fight to get hold of my breath.

The orgasm surges through my body, completely taking over me until I'm left moaning his name and revelling in the satisfaction, he has just given me.

Jacob eagerly stares at my weak body recovering from his tongue. He enjoys watching me in this state. He loves knowing what he can do to me. As I glance down to meet with his eyes, I can see the smugness all over his face.

"Are you ready for your hot chocolate now?" he whispers, but to his surprise I shake my head before gathering myself to my knees.

"Sit," I demand as I point at the bar stool. His eyes glance towards it before gazing back at me.

He smirks but does as he is told.

"I'm sick of how smug you are," I say as I follow behind him.

I keep my eyes fixed on him as I lower myself in between his legs.

"I just like to see you vulnerable." He smiles but this time with a slightly heavier breath. I know he is growing aroused now with anticipation, just as I was.

"Me too," I simply answer before sliding my tongue down the shaft of his thick length.

Instantly he grips the stool with one hand and the other hand grips into my hair.

The sound of his breathing getting faster and wilder turns me on all over again. Even I'm surprised at how passionately I take him into my mouth. Somehow, Jacob can turn me into a version of myself I have never known. I have no self-control with Jacob, no rules, and fuck, let's be honest, no morals. I just can't help myself. I suck faster and deeper as I allow him to hit the back of my throat.

I'm consumed by this erotic whirlwind and I can't stop.

"Fuck, Mia!" he pants as my tongue swirls all around his most sensitive part until I feel him tighten.

I whine passionately as he grips my hair harder, pushing my head deeper onto him just as I feel his hips thrust and him spill into the back of my throat.

I welcome the taste.

I watch him collapse back into the stool as he catches his breath and now it's me who is smiling with smugness. The tables have turned.

Chapter thirty-four

My legs are still a bit wobbly, but I do my best to pull myself together in the bathroom. As I get myself back into my clothes, my phone drops out of my jeans pocket, revealing my lit screen.

Two missed calls.

They're from Alex. Shit, I've been so caught up in Jacob I had completely forgotten he was being discharged soon. But surely, it's not yet? I was certain it would be after the weekend at least.

I splash cold water on my face from the bathroom sink and prepare myself to call him. I creep over to the bathroom door to make sure Jacob isn't in ear shot but thankfully he is still down in the kitchen.

Before I even have the chance to call him back my phone suddenly vibrates in my hand.

"Hello?" I whisper.

"Mia?" Alex's voice sounds concerned.

"Yes."

"Why are you whispering?"

"I... I just woke up," I lie. "Are you okay?"

"Oh. Yeah, I'm okay thank you. I can come home. Well, to yours, if that's still okay?"

Oh shit.

I didn't think Alex coming to stay would be a problem considering only a few days ago I didn't think I'd be continuing things with Jacob. I can't just blow him off now though, I couldn't do that to him. I promised him and I can't just leave him in the lurch. I mean, where would he even go?

"It's not is it?" His dejected voice interrupts my anxieties.

"Shit! Sorry Alex. I was just distracted. Of course, it's absolutely fine. Are you ready now?"

"Yeah…if you're sure. I don't want to ruin any plans you have."

"No, you're fine! Don't worry. I'll leave in five minutes okay. See you soon," I say, trying to sound convincing.

As soon as I hang up the phone, I bring my hands up to my face.

"Fuuuck!" I whisper through gritted teeth to myself.

Okay. Okay, think of a plan, Mia.

I don't want to but I'm going to have to lie to Jacob, at least for now. I can't go downstairs now after our day together and tell him I'm off to pick up my ex-husband so he can come and live with me for a while. That'll go down like the *Titanic*.

Fuck, but I don't want to lie either. I love what I'm building with Jacob. But on the other hand, I know he won't understand. He thinks Alex is a piece of shit from what I have told him and there's just no way he'll accept this.

Annoyed, I pace back and forth around the bathroom, battling with my own thoughts. I hate situations like this, I can never work out what is best to do. I'm so torn.

"Mia?" Jacob calls from the bottom of the stairs.

Bollocks.

"Coming!" I call as panic sets in.

I rush down the stairs hurriedly so Jacob can see something has changed.

"I have to go," I blurt, as soon as my eyes meet his.

"Huh?"

"It's my...cousin. He took an overdose and there's no one else. I have to go to him."

Jacob stares at me bewildered. Trying to process what I'm saying.

"What? Where?" he replies.

"I have to get him from the hospital. He'll probably have to stay with me for a little while."

I feel so guilty deceiving him but it's the only way we can avoid the drama.

"You better be joking Mia, it's like eight o'clock at night now? And it's pouring down. Most of the roads around here will be flooded by now! You can't drive. Not in this."

"I'll be fine, I'm sure I can find a way around any floods."

"No, it could be dangerous. I'll take you," he responds authoritatively as he grabs his jacket.

"I have to go on my own Jacob. Sorry. He is very embarrassed about what's happened, and he won't be able to cope being around somebody he doesn't know right now. I'm sorry but I'm going on my own," I awkwardly reply. I can barely make eye contact now and I feel like I'm being so transparent.

"Mia, it's fucking dangerous out there. The winds are picking up, the rain is too heavy..."

"I'll call you when I'm back home to let you know I'm safe," I quickly cut him off and turn to leave.

"This is bullshit! Mia! Stop!" Jacob shouts behind me.

"I'll call you!" I repeat and I rush to my car as quickly as I can to avoid any further confrontation.

The guilt is unbearable as I drive away and see Jacob still standing at his front door in my rear-view mirror. He looks confused and pissed off.

Just as I pull away, I see him waving his arms at me to stop, but I can't stop. I made a promise to Alex and as much as I wish he didn't, he really needs my help right now. Within seconds I pull out of our cul-de-sac and Jacob is no longer in my view.

1 new message - Jacob flashes up on my screen before I have even made it to the main road, but I can't open it. I have to concentrate on the roads. I'll call him soon and hopefully once he knows I'm back home and safe he'll be fine.

Jacob was right about the floods, they're everywhere and it's too hard to see them in the dark. I'm worried my car won't get through them all, but I keep going and just hope for the best.

The wind whistles harshly through the vents in the car and the rain hammers so loudly on my windscreen that it's deafening. I'd be lying if I said it wasn't scary. Thankfully, hardly any cars are on the road which makes it a little more manageable, but the unpredictability of the roads is overwhelming.

I keep an eye on the satnav and I'm grateful every time I get through another mile. The drive is taking twice as long though because I'm having to go so slowly.

Just when I think I'm over the worst of it, I clock some blue flashing lights up ahead and realise I'm joining the back of a very long queue of traffic.

As my car edges closer at a snail's pace, I realise firefighters are helping stranded cars from the floods.

Oh god. This is going to take hours.

I send Alex a quick text message to let him know I'm going to be a while because of how bad the roads have become. The traffic is at a complete standstill now. I promised Jacob I would text him when I got home but at this rate it'll be gone midnight.

Reluctantly, my thumb finds Jacob's message. I'm almost worried to open it in case he is mad at me, but I can't ignore it either.

Mia, I don't really understand what's going on...I'm sorry your cousin isn't well, but you've become my whole world and I hate to think of you out in this. Please, please just drive safely. Call me as soon as you can.

I smile at the warmth in his words although I think they've made me feel worse for running out on him in the way that I have and only telling him a half truth.

Eventually, the traffic starts to move again, albeit very slowly but at least it's something.

Twelve more miles until I reach the hospital and I can ring Jacob and let him know he was right about the roads, but I managed halfway and I'm safe.

Chapter thirty-five

The car journey back with Alex has been a bit odd to say the least. It feels as though he is trying to recreate what we had when we first started dating – he's a little flirtatious, overly complimenting me and generally trying too hard. I could be over-thinking this, I am over-tired after all. I didn't get to Alex until almost midnight and I feel wiped out after sitting for so long in that traffic. Thankfully the roads seem to be clearing so the rest of the journey should only be half the time.

"I can drive if you want me to?" Alex suggests, sweetly.

"Oh no, I'll be fine. Come on, you've literally just got out of hospital, I don't expect you to drive. Plus, you don't know the way," I say with a smile.

No point in trying to ignore the elephant in the room. These are some strange circumstances. My ex-husband is about to walk into my new home that I've worked for in my new life. As much as we are trying to front it out, it's clearly going to be somewhat awkward to say the least.

"Fine. I'll cook breakfast in the morning then to say thank you."

I nod politely and give him another reassuring smile but inside I'm struggling a little bit. It's hard trying to keep a conversation flowing with somebody I have so much history with but also thought I'd never speak to again. And, of course, I have Jacob on my mind. I won't be able to keep Alex a secret forever – eventually Jacob will realise who the man is in my house and I'm not entirely sure how he'll react. He isn't as understanding as I am.

I don't expect him to be happy about it, but I do hope he can just accept the fact that this is my decision and I know what I'm doing.

My thoughts keep my brain busy long enough that before I know it, I'm pulling into my driveway. It's such a relief to finally be home. I notice quickly that there are still lights on over at Jacob's house. I don't want him to come over so to put him off I quickly send a text message just to let him know I'm home and safe, but also really tired. I let him know I'll speak to him in the morning and add some kisses before hitting send.

"A house with all the glass. Just like you said you always wanted," Alex says softly as he climbs out of the car and stares at my new home.

"Yeah...it's awesome in the daylight."

"I bet..." Alex politely agrees but I do feel like I'm picking up on some sadness in his voice.

It mustn't be easy for him. After the divorce I wanted us to both find our way onto a new path and be happy, but so far, it's clear that it's only me who has managed it. I feel so sad for him. I want to hug him, but I don't want to blur the lines. I don't want him to think anything more than a friendship could ever happen between us now. I have to stay conscious of that.

"I have a futon that I'm supposed to be collecting from the store on Monday. I thought it would be better than the sofa. I'm sorry it's not here already – I didn't expect you so soon," I explain as Alex looks around the living room.

"That's fine. I can just sleep on the sofa tonight, it's not a big deal," Alex assures me, and I smile gratefully.

"Okay, great. Well, I'll grab you some bedding and extra pillows and I'll help you get set up. It's so late, I'm sure all you want to do is sleep."

"Actually, all I want to do is talk to you. But these painkillers are going to make me sleep either way. So yeah, I best get sorted on the sofa," he jokes, and his eyes light up as I giggle back.

I notice Alex hasn't got any clothes with him and I remember the fire. He must have lost everything.

I don't want Jacob to see me leaving the house with Alex tomorrow, but we really do need to go shopping. He can't sleep and live in one pair of jeans. The earlier the better for us, that way we hopefully won't be seen.

"Shall we head out early tomorrow? I thought I'd set my alarm and we can get up and get out at the crack of dawn. There's a really good outlet near us, we can get you some clothes and essentials," I offer, but really, I'm insisting, and I think Alex can tell.

"Um, sure. Bright and early it is. I'll see you tomorrow." He smiles thankfully and I disappear upstairs to get the extra bedding.

It doesn't take me to long to gather everything together but by the time I come back downstairs, Alex has made me a cup of tea which he has left on the kitchen counter.

"For me?"

"Yeah, well, it's freezing and horrible out there and after driving all that way for me, the least I can do is fix you a hot drink," he says gently.

As I walk over to the counter to retrieve my tea, I can feel Alex's eyes heavily on me. I glance up to be sure and just as I do, I catch his gaze. His eyes narrow as he takes everything in – takes the new me in.

"I don't think I have ever seen you look so beautiful, Mia. You seem so happy here."

"It's just nice to be settled." I shrug. "It's not all perfect. My best friend is a stray cat."

"Your best friend?" Alex smirks.

"Well actually, my only friend." I laugh, which makes his smirk grow into a full smile.

It's actually really nice to see him smile so brightly.

"I wish I had seen that," he continues as he throws his head back with a chuckle.

"Well I can easily paint you a picture if you want? Just imagine a sweaty dishevelled Mia, tired from moving all day. I didn't have time to eat anything so after two glasses of wine, I was pissed and telling a cat my life story. She probably only keeps coming back because she feels sorry for me!"

"Tragic!" Alex teases, but suddenly his bright smile fades and the banter between us feels as though it's been sucked out of the room. Instead he stares at me intently and I notice quickly that his eyes are watering.

He drops his head and rubs the back of his neck before staring back at me, looking so defeated.

"I should have never let you go, Mia," he finally whispers.

Chapter thirty-six

"I think I met your friend last night by the way," Alex says, probably to fill the silence in the car.

"Oh really?"

"Yeah. The stray cat you were talking about."

"Oh!" I giggle.

"She was scratching at the door, so I left her a bit of tuna and water. She's cute."

"Yeah she is. She's great company." I smile.

Neither one of us has mentioned last night, which was fine, but now that we're heading back home again, I'm really starting to feel awkward.

We got up early and pretty much hit the road straightaway. Alex was a little reluctant to shop for anything – I think he was a little embarrassed that he doesn't have much money these days and was probably trying to keep it polite too. But I happily took the lead and helped him get a few pairs of jeans, t-shirts, jumpers, hygiene stuff, pretty much all the basics. He kept thanking me and I know he is grateful. I feel like it's the right thing to help him, but I worry deep down that he is hoping for more and the last thing I want to do is to lead him on or hurt his feelings.

"Who's that?" Alex asks, pointing to my phone in the holder next to the steering wheel.

I instantly notice that it's another phone call coming through from Jacob. I missed two of his calls earlier whilst we were in the shops and I know I really need to answer it and let him know I'm fine, but I feel too uncomfortable to talk to him in front of Alex.

I won't be able to keep everything a secret for much longer and it's best all round if I at least let Alex know that I'm not available for a relationship.

"About last night..." I randomly say, like word vomit. I wasn't actually ready to talk; it just came out. I'm not even sure what to say next and now I'm awkwardly stuttering.

"I know," Alex interrupts, almost as if to reassure me. "I shouldn't have said that. The last thing I want is for things to get weird between us. I'm sorry."

"Thank you." I sigh with relief.

I'm pleased he said that because hopefully now the rest will be easier to explain. It would be easy to leave the conversation here, but I know I have to be a bit more open with him, he needs to know that absolutely nothing can or will happen between us.

"Alex, the guy on my phone just now is somebody I'm seeing," I say as a swarm of butterflies fill my stomach and not in a good way. I suddenly feel like I do when I'm about to get in the dentist chair: sick, nervous and filled with dread. This is definitely a discussion I never thought I'd be having with my ex-husband.

Alex doesn't respond much. He continues staring out of the windscreen and into the distance as if he is processing what I said. I can understand that the news might be bringing him mixed emotions and perhaps he isn't sure what to say, but my god, the silence is brutal.

"I thought you should know because I wouldn't want us to get our wires crossed over what is happening here. We can only be friends now," I follow up with. I probably don't need to say any-thing more, and I could just be making it worse for him, but I tend to babble when I'm nervous.

"That was a bit quick," he speaks up, bluntly.

Oh god. Just hearing his tone of voice has made things a hundred times more awkward.

"Yes, it happened a lot quicker than I ever imagined," I say softly, trying to somewhat agree with him. "I honestly thought it would just be me and the stray cat for the next ten years. But sometimes things just happen, unexpectedly, don't they?"

Alex sharply exhales in a way that lets me know he is pissed off and shakes his head in disbelief.

"Who is he then?" he asks, begrudgingly.

Shit. I can't say who he is. I can't let him know it's my neighbour, it'll only make him feel worse. Plus, I'm not exactly proud of it. I don't have to tell him *everything.* At this point, he should just appreciate that I'm choosing to even be *this* open with him. I'm surely entitled to keep the rest to myself.

"He's someone I met through work. A new guy, so you wouldn't have ever met him," I say, trying to sound as convincing as pos-sible.

"Oh. Okay, well you deserve to be happy," he responds, his words a lot less harsh than before. "It is what it is."

"Thank you, Alex. I appreciate that, I really do. I don't want to hurt you, I just needed to be honest."

"Yep. And you've done that. But if you don't mind, I'd rather we changed the subject, respectfully."

I nod sympathetically but absolutely no new topic of conversation springs to mind. Instead all I can think about is how awkward the rest of his stay is going to be. I thought he was okay but the way he said the last word made it clear he is hurt inside. Which is the last thing I wanted to do.

I feel like we could probably do with a little space apart. I could sit upstairs in my bedroom for a couple of hours, but I think that would only make it so obvious and worse than it is now.

"Why don't I drop you back and I'll go to the supermarket and get us dinner?" I suggest, forcing a casual approach.

"Sure." Alex simply nods.

"Cool. Any requests?"

"I used to love it when you made homemade ravioli. It was probably one of my favourite dishes you ever cooked. Could we have that? If it's not too much trouble?" he asks me with a downcast look in his eyes.

"Of course!" I say a little too enthusiastically, but I'm really trying to cheer him up.

"Thanks. To be honest, I'm glad to be going back to yours for a while anyway. I'm feeling really tired. I might have a little lie down whilst you're out."

"Oh yeah, that's understandable. You should definitely get some rest and I'll go and pick up the ingredients. If you're asleep when I get back, I'll just wake you up when dinner's ready."

"Thank you, Mia. I appreciate all you've done and as soon as I can I'll be out of your hair and leave you to live your life," he says quietly, just as we pull up to the front of my house.

"I can still be your friend and help you for as long as you need me to," I say, trying to sound positive and encouraging as Alex reaches for the car door to get out.

He doesn't say anything more but just nods gratefully although I can clearly see the dejected look in his face. I know I shouldn't, but I feel horrendously guilty.

Maybe having him here wasn't the best idea after all. Maybe our lives are just too different now. They always say that when a couple break up there's always one who wasn't quite ready for it to end. I think this may have been too soon for Alex. As much as he needed someone to help, as much as he needed me, I worry it's going to do more harm than good.

Chapter thirty-seven

"Hey," I say shyly with my phone anxiously pressed against my ear.

"Hey! What is going on? Where have you been?" Jacob responds in a concerned but almost possessive manner.

"I had to take my cousin shopping today, he had hardly any belongings with him."

"And you couldn't answer my phone calls in front of him?" Jacob fires back, irritation thick in his voice.

"I, I didn't hear it," I stutter anxiously. I can feel myself growing more tangled in this web of lies I have created for myself and I hate it.

"Why the fuck are you lying to me, Mia?"

"Huh? About what?"

"About the fucking for sale sign that has gone up at the front of your house. That's why I was trying to ring. To find out what is going on. Why didn't you tell me? I don't understand!" he growls angrily but the emotion strains his voice and somehow, I can picture how upset he is.

Fuck, I didn't even notice any sign when I dropped Alex off and I totally forgot that I even made those plans. I have been so caught up with the on and off relationship between Jacob and me that I completely buried any thought of me leaving.

"Jacob, I can explain all of that," I say, trying to speak over him.

"I think it tells me everything I need to know, Mia. I can't fucking believe you! I'm about to leave my wife and you're planning on packing up and moving away without even telling me?! What the fuck!" he explodes.

"Jacob, I…"

"Fuck this, we were supposed to be a team."

"We are! Jacob, I promise we are. I had a wobble and I just thought…"

"No, no, don't you dare try to justify it like that!" Jacob interrupts. "A wobble is maybe panicking and needing me to reassure you, a wobble is not putting your fucking house up for sale and leaving me!"

"Okay, okay…it was more than a wobble. I got scared, I am scared. I'm scared of all of this Jacob. I'm scared that I played this dangerous game and now I'm in too deep. People are going to get hurt and I'm scared!" I scream as tears spill from my eyes just like my anxieties are spilling over in this conversation.

"You can't just turn the waterworks on, Mia. Imagine how my morning has been – and you couldn't even be bothered to answer a call."

"I'm sorry, you're right. I didn't think…" I wipe the tears and try to plead with him to understand that I really didn't mean to hurt him.

"I'm done, Mia, I am fucking done. I'm sorry too. I knew I wasn't cut out for this bullshit. Too many feelings make life way too hard. I was better off the way I was. I'm better off not feeling this bullshit way for people."

"You don't mean that? I'm not going anywhere, Jacob. I promise you."

"How can I believe that now? I'm done. I'm so done," he mutters disappointedly before the phone line goes dead.

I can instantly feel a migraine coming on. How have I let his happen?

I can't imagine how confused and hurt I would feel if I thought he was suddenly leaving me and keeping secrets, but I do wish he had let me explain a bit more. Maybe I could have helped him to see my thought process. I feel so stupid now though. Why couldn't I have just remembered to phone the estate agents and pull out of everything? How could I let something so important slip my mind?

I'm shaking sitting in the car. I just want to drive straight to Jacob's house now and explain how I was feeling at the time and to reassure him that the way I feel now is different. I want to tell him how strong my feelings are for him. I want to make him see that I am in this for the long haul. Then he'd wrap his arms around me tightly and just be with me. He'd forgive me and kiss me and hold me. I need that desperately right now, but I won't go to his house, not yet. I have to give him space to calm down first and then maybe, hopefully, I can talk to him tomorrow.

I feel so fed up walking around the supermarket, I can barely concentrate on what ingredients I need, but I take my time. I'm in no rush to get back home right now. Alex will probably be asleep anyway and to be honest I am enjoying the space.

I peruse the beauty aisle a bit longer than usual. I think I'll give myself a little pamper tonight and have a long soak in the tub before heading off for an early night. I throw some products into the trolley without really seeing what they are, but they look decent enough. I'll welcome anything that can help me out of this shitty mood I'm now in.

I painfully avoid the ice cream aisle like the plague, I can't keep turning to Ben and Jerry's every time I'm feeling this glum, I'll end up with back rolls by next month otherwise.

By the time I load up the car with my shopping and begin my drive home it's pretty much dark and getting cold again. I'm looking forward to my bubble bath. I'm pretty sure it's the only thing that will help ease my migraine.

As I pull into our little cul-de-sac, I subtly glance over towards Jacob's house. Most of the lights are off apart from the one in his study. I guess he is catching up on some work. The window of his study brings back instant memories of our first-ever passionate encounter. I love the memory and it makes me smile but it's bittersweet now – the thought gives me both butterflies and pain. I miss him already.

"There she is!" Alex loudly booms down the hallway as I walk through the front door.

I know. Instantly, I know. He's drunk. The house looks a little untidy and music blares from the speaker in the kitchen. His eyes are glazed, and they look unkind. Just like they used to when we were married, and he drank too much and spent the night drunkenly yelling at me about how everything that had gone wrong in his life was down to me. I feel sick in the pit of my stomach.

"Alex? Are you drunk?" I ask, despite knowing the answer.

"I've poured you a glass! Come drink with me Mia, let's say cheers to your new relationship," he says in a way that makes me feel on edge.

Another fuck up of mine. I forgot to hide the alcohol. As soon as I step into the kitchen, I quickly spot that my bottle of vodka is empty, and he has moved onto the red wine.

"Alex...You shouldn't be drinking," I say and grab the bottle of wine from the counter.

I drop the shopping bags on the floor and head over to the sink to tip the rest of the wine away, but he quickly steps in front of me and snatches the bottle out of my hand before taking a glass of red wine from the counter and handing it to me.

"Where were we? Oh yeah, cheers to...What's his name?" He smirks but his eyes are filled with hatred.

"It's not important! Alex, you are supposed to be sober. You can't drink in my house."

"Okay...I won't drink another drop if you promise to stop whoring yourself about, deal?"

"You're being pathetic!" I snap. "I'm not talking to you like this, go and sleep it off."

I grab the shopping bags and begin piling everything into the fridge and cupboards. I do my best to manoeuvre around the kitchen without making eye contact with him.

I can't allow myself to get drawn into some head-to-head petty argument.

"Come on, one drink...for old time's sake?" he slurs as he pushes the glass of wine back into my hand. I only take it to stop him from spilling it everywhere.

"I have a migraine, Alex. I just want a bath and bed. I'm not doing this with you. Sleep it off," I say with authority, but inside I'm becoming scared of him.

His look is colder than I have ever seen it before, and I can't see him letting this go.

"Okay, fine," he eventually says after staring at me for the longest time. "How about one fuck...for old time's sake?"

His eyes darken as he takes a step towards me, backing me into the wall. Somehow, he looks bigger, taller than before. His shoulders have tensed up and broadened as he takes another step towards me.

"Take your clothes off, Mia."

Chapter thirty-eight

My mouth is dry, and I feel physically sick. I had always been worried about what Alex could be capable of, but I never thought I would have to worry now that I had removed myself from that situation. I thought I had made myself safe. I didn't think this would be a concern anymore.

"Alex, stop this now. You aren't this person!" I shout.

"How would you know what person I am, Mia? You fucking left me and didn't look back. All you cared about was your fucking self!"

"That's not true! I cared for you too, but our marriage was broken, you were broken, and you wouldn't let me fix you. I'm sorry!" I cry and I realise my whole body is trembling.

"Fix me!? You really are an arrogant little bitch! Look at you, living in your pathetic suburban house – you really think you're a somebody don't you? You're NOTHING!" he roars so loud I'm left with ringing in my ears.

"I'm sorry! I'm so sorry," I sob, growing terrified of his erratic anger. "Please stop this. I just wanted to help. I am so sorry!"

"You swan into my hospital room, looking at me with pity in your eyes. You see me as nothing but a joke, don't you? And the second I tell you I still care about you; you brag about having some new man! You just couldn't WAIT to throw that in my face, could you?"

I watch as his fists clench and his face grow redder with every word, he growls at me.

"No! No, I swear, it wasn't like that. I just didn't want to hurt you. Please Alex, just take a moment to calm down. This isn't you, it's the vodka talking. I know you better than this Alex. Please stop this now and we can forget all about it..."

With that, Alex slumps down on the sofa with his head in his hands. I daren't move from the wall or make a sound. I'm still shaking, and my breathing is fast and out of control. I feel as though I could have a panic attack, but I try to remain calm and quiet. If I can get him to calm down just a little, I might be able to diffuse this.

Alex takes a large gulp of his red wine before placing it onto the coffee table in front of him and looking up at me. His eyes feel cold and unforgiving.

"You broke my heart Mia and then you broke the rest of me. Maybe I wasn't perfect, but I loved you, I loved who you were, before you turned into this bitch."

"I'm sorry," I whisper.

His anger is so up and down, I really have no idea how I can handle him anymore. I wish I knew how to calm him down but with each spiteful word he says to me, I realise that I barely know him at all.

Crazy how you can be married to a person and they can still feel like a complete stranger.

"I need you to give our marriage another chance. I need you to tell me you're sorry. I need you to promise me you're going to stop being so fucking selfish and I need you to love me," he announces, and his eyes fixate onto me, awaiting my response.

I steady myself against the wall, trying to keep my balance. I feel like I could just pass out. I haven't felt like this since the night he smashed up our house, but the familiarity comes back all too easily.

"I can be your friend. I can be here as long as you need me," I offer timidly.

He lets out a horrifically fake chuckle before standing up in full rage and throwing the wine glass forcefully in my direction. It misses the side of my head by an inch and smashes on the wall next to me. I scream in panic. The stain of the red wine all over my white wall and the shattered pieces of glass around me do nothing to snap him out of his rage. If anything, he glares at me unsatisfied – he's only just begun.

"Alex, stop!" I plead, but it's too late. Before the cries even leave my mouth, he has turned to the kitchen and instantly starts to rip cupboard doors off their hinges. He swipes his hands across the shelves until all my cups and glasses are smashing against my tiled floor.

"You stuck-up ugly whore!" he bellows before grabbing the photo frames from my dresser and throwing them around the room.

"NO!" I scream as I spot my favourite photograph of my dad high above his head and he readies himself to smash it in front of me.

"Please, Alex! My dad gave me that frame, please!"

My desperate cries seem to give him the kick he needs because a hateful smile spreads across his face the second he realises he has found my Achilles heel. He now knows how to hurt me, and he revels in the moment whilst he holds my most sentimental item high into the air and laughs as he watches me hopelessly beg him.

My eyes pause for a split second on the photo of my dad wrapping his arms around me on the beach a few weeks before he passed away and instantly my heart drops into my stomach and, without thought, I lunge towards him and attempt to snatch the frame out of his hand.

The next thing I know, I'm on the floor with blood dripping from my cheekbone. It takes me a second or two to realise that Alex just used the frame to strike me hard across the face. I lean on my elbow as I try to pull myself up from the floor; my cheek radiates heat and the photo frame I tried to save is in pieces around me anyway.

"Shit, Mia! I'm so sorry. You wound me up, but I'm so sorry," he breathes, panicked, as he climbs on top of me and attempts to cradle me. I'm ready to scream but at that second, I see a familiar black trainer fly above my head and slam into Alex's face.

The kick throws Alex back and straight off me and he slumps against the side of my sofa.

It's Jacob.

"Oh god," I sob as the relief of knowing I'm now safe overwhelms me.

I'm ready for Jacob to scoop me into his arms and take me away from this, but he too looks as enraged as Alex did moments ago. He barely notices me. His eyes are locked onto Alex and he is gunning for him.

Jacob strides towards him and effortlessly pulls him to his feet and slams him against the wall where the wine glass was smashed. He grips him by the neck, and he looks wildly at him and then back at me.

"This is him, isn't it?" Jacob fiercely yells and I nod as I keep one hand pressed against my bloodied cheek.

Jacob furiously slams his head hard against the wall before throwing a punch. And another.

Alex deserves it, but Jacob doesn't deserve to go to prison for him. I throw myself in front of Jacob and as I remove my hand from my cheek to hold him back, his eyes widen as he notices the full impact Alex had on my face.

I can see in his eyes that I'm his priority now.

He instantly cups my swollen cheek in his palm and his eyes go from wild and angry to soft but sad puppy dog eyes.

I turn back to see a shocked Alex wobble to his feet.

He looks utterly blind-sided to have someone fight back.

"Now get out!" I shout.

I hold myself together and stand tall as he grabs his jacket and phone and clumsily heads out of my front door.

The second he disappears out of my vision, my shoulders drop, and my knees buckle beneath me. Now that he is gone, I allow the fear, the pain and everything else I have put up with to take over me and I drop to my knees and sob into my hands.

Chapter thirty-nine

It's been four hours since Alex attacked me, and I have only just managed to get myself up off the floor. Jacob stayed with me the whole time. He tried desperately to persuade me to go to the hospital and get checked out, but I kept saying that I was far too embarrassed to go.

I was anxious to open up about everything. I wasn't sure if I was going to have another argument on my hands once Jacob realised that my cousin was actually my ex-husband, but he just seemed to understand. Even if he is angry, he cares about me too much to show it now.

He just nodded and listened, and I explained why I did everything I did and how foolish I have been. I sobbed and told him how sorry I was, and he apologised too. He told me how he was coming over to make up with me about our earlier argument on the phone and that's when he heard the shouting and all the chaos.

Sweetly, he told me to have a long hot bath whilst he cleaned up for me downstairs. I protested a little, it's my mess after all. The shattered glass and red-stained walls all too clearly display the repercussions of my stupidity and I don't expect Jacob to clean up after that, but he insisted, and I did as he asked.

I cringe when I wipe away the steam from the bathroom mirror and catch a glimpse of my swollen cheek. The huge lump looks like a golf ball– it's disgusting and makes me feel sick. I can't even tolerate the injury scenes in *Grey's Anatomy*, and I know they're fake. I have never been great with blood or wounds and seeing such a fresh gash across my disfigured cheekbone fills me with anxiety, and the reality of knowing it was caused by a man I shared my life with hurts me worse than the wound itself.

Whether I like it or not, a valuable lesson has been learned tonight. That's one positive to come out of this disaster. I'll never help somebody who can't be helped again. My dad used to warn me of these types of encounters, he'd tell me that some people in life expect more than just a wife or a husband, they expect a full-time carer, a therapist and sometimes a punch bag. And it won't matter how you try to save these people, or help them, he would say, they will always pull you down before they pick themselves up. Some people are simply willing to take more than you can give.

My skin feels extra sensitive as I immerse myself into the warm water and the second I lay my head back to relax, I instantly feel the throb in my cheekbone. It's like having an extra heartbeat in your face. It's not a good feeling at all and I'm struggling to relax.

I squeeze the warm sponge over my body and gently wipe away the evening. I notice a few bruises appearing on my arms and on my hips, probably from where I fell onto the floor.

I climb carefully out of the bath and wrap a white towel around me and pull my hair back into a low bun. I tiptoe into my bedroom but keep the lights off and light one scented candle instead; my eyes can't handle any more brightness than that right now.

"Hey, that was quick," Jacob says softly as he appears in the doorway.

"I couldn't get comfortable," I answer as I lie back onto my bed.

"How are you feeling?"

"Sore," I say which makes Jacob's head drop guiltily.

"Please don't look like that, you've done nothing wrong."

"I just wish I was here sooner, before that waste of oxygen had a chance to hurt you."

"I'll be fine – in a few days, I will be good as new," I say to reassure him from his guilt. If it wasn't for Jacob, things could have been ten times worse. He saved me tonight and he has absolutely nothing to feel guilty for.

Jacob's head drops down and a sorrowful sigh is all that fills the room.

"Look at your face though."

I offer half a smile; I'm not sure what to say.

"Where else does it hurt?" he asks as he sits beside me on my bed.

"Here..." I quietly reply as I gently gesture over my hips.

Jacob carefully takes a hold of my white towel and opens it up to reveal my dampened naked body.

I feel a little vulnerable like this but safe, nonetheless.

Jacob's hand carefully glides up to my hips and he traces the marks very gently with his thumb, before lowering himself and placing soft kisses against my hip bone.

"And here..." I whisper and point to my ribs. His eyes look up at me briefly with his mouth still slightly apart and he drops his head back down onto my ribs. He places gentle kisses on them and slowly makes his way to my breasts.

"Where else?" he whispers.

"Just here," I respond and cup my painful cheek.

Slowly and carefully, Jacob climbs on top of me and his lips part as he seductively but lovingly kisses away my pain.

"And here…" I mumble as my finger grazes my bottom lip and I stare at him, achingly waiting for his lips to touch mine.

I welcome the warmth of his lips against mine and open my mouth to allow his tongue to slide over mine.

With his lips still against mine, I tug at his white t-shirt and begin pulling it up to his shoulders; his hand meets mine and together we pull it up and over his head.

I lie back whilst Jacob plants gentle kisses on every bruise and mark on my skin again and holds my hand as he does.

My body feels so relaxed now; the trembling has stopped, and I feel the safest I have ever felt, lying beneath him.

Carefully he leans up and I help him remove his grey joggers. He is so careful with me and I love him all the more for it.

My legs part as he guides himself back on top of me and quickly, I feel him deep inside me and all my aches and pains seem to fade whilst passion and relief rush through me instead. This is the release I have needed today. To feel Jacob loving me in a way nobody else can.

Satisfied moans spill from my lips and as I arch my neck, I realise I can see our naked bodies in the reflection of my bedroom window. I joyfully watch on as Jacob attentively and tenderly penetrates me. His hands run all over my body, taking in every inch of me.

I hold onto him tightly, enjoying the protectiveness I feel with his broad body on top of me.

Our soft moans begin to sync up and I feel Jacob's gentle rhythm quicken until I feel his release inside of me.

I tug hard at his hair as I join him and finally our eyes lock onto each other's as we catch our breath again.

Chapter forty

I haven't seen Puss lately and to be honest, I really miss her. I could have really done with her company this past week. It's been three days since Alex attacked me and my swelling has reduced somewhat but it's still very noticeable and my body still aches.

Elle arrived back yesterday, and I asked Jacob to wait just a day or two more to tell her, just because I really need the extra time to get my head straight before the storm arrives.

Although it will take a little time, I am so ready to lead a quieter life now with Jacob. No more drama, no more getting our wires crossed, no more upset, no ex-husbands and definitely no Elle. Just a new beginning and a new relationship and a real chance to be happy.

This is probably the most selfish thing I have ever thought to myself, well, in respect to Elle anyway. But I know in my heart that Elle doesn't love Jacob. I know I'm not stealing the love of her life – her unlimited credit card maybe, but not her true love. I'm sure there are plenty of other wealthy men she can leech off.

I have been for a stroll around the country fields for the past hour, even though my ribs and hip still ache, it's important I keep moving. I think it helped. When I return to my front door, I'm saddened by what I see. The bowl of food and cat biscuits I left out for Puss is still untouched. This is so unlike her; I hope she's safe and hasn't been injured or anything. She's not even officially my cat but I'm starting to really worry for her. She's been my only friend since I moved here, and I feel like I'm missing a piece of me without her around.

"Mia..." Jacob startles me as he appears from the corner.

"Jacob?! We shouldn't be seen..."

"Elle sent me," he quickly interrupts. "She wants me to invite you over for dinner tonight. It'll be awkward as hell, not to mention quite cruel considering. Are you sure you don't want me to tell her now?"

"I... I don't know. I'm just not ready. I still feel weak and just not myself. I'm not sure I can go through it just yet," I stutter.

"Fuck. Okay then, we'll have to put ourselves through a dinner..."

"Sorry..." I mumble.

"I understand that you need a few more days but then I really have to tell her, okay?"

I nod in agreement as Jacob begins walking back to his house.

"Oh, come over for seven!" he calls back before disappearing through his front door.

Fuck. Dinner with Elle. I guess this is my new normal now. Dinner with my boyfriend's wife...Wow. Someone sign me up for therapy now. It would be comical what I have gotten myself into – well, if it wasn't happening in real life anyway.

My afternoon is now spent clock watching, counting the minutes until I have to head over for dinner. The time is going painfully slowly. I just want to get it over and done with, but time seems to be taking forever.

I head upstairs and browse through my wardrobe, desperately looking for something that doesn't scream "I'm guilty" or "hope Cape Verde was nice, apologies for shagging your husband".

My eyes roll at the sarcastic thoughts that are jumping through my mind. To be fair, it's always been a coping mechanism, I did the same at my dad's funeral. It was easier to joke than to fall apart.

As I jump in the shower and get myself ready, I desperately keep trying to remind myself that I'm a good person, although it isn't easy.

Sometimes good people do bad things, but it doesn't make them the same as bad people who do bad things, my dad used to say.

Looking back, I'm pretty sure he said that to defend my mum, who wasn't exactly living by her wedding vows.

I give my hair a bouncy blow dry when I'm out of the shower and I eventually decide on a black jumpsuit to wear. It's classy and not at all revealing. The more reserved the better, I think. Although I do opt for red lipstick – red is confidence and I need that by the bucketload tonight.

A few sprays of a classic Estée Lauder perfume that Mum sent me from duty free and I'm ready, sort of, for an evening of awkwardness and dread. Fantastic.

I may as well be dragging my feet I'm walking that slowly across the gravel and up their driveway.

Well Mia, I think to myself, you made your bed. You've got to lie in it.

"Mia!" Elle screeches loudly and exaggeratedly, as always.

"Hey!" I reply, doing my best to mimic her excitement.

"Jesus…your cheek, Mia! What happened?" she gasps as she spots my bruise from Alex.

"Oh, nothing serious. Just me being clumsy," I say, trying to shrug it off.

"Oh dear! Well, come and sit down. I'll get Jakey to fix you a drink, sweetie."

I hate it when she calls him Jakey, I absolutely cringe inside.

I'm ushered into the kitchen where the dining table has been exquisitely set up, although I wouldn't expect anything less.

"Here darling, I brought back this sparkling wine from the hotel, it really is delicious. You'll love it!" She smiles brightly as she fills my glass flute to the brim with wine.

"Thank you. It's nice," I politely say after taking a sip.

"Ah, yay! I knew you'd love it. It's only cheap stuff so I knew instantly it would suit your palette." She says it so flippantly, I have no idea how to take it. From most people, that would be considered insulting and rude, but Elle usually makes remarks that she seems to think are appropriate, so I have no idea whether this is just one of those.

I awkwardly laugh it off. Elle's rudeness should be the least of my worries.

Elle dashes around the kitchen as she pours soup into bowls and cheerfully hums as she does so. I half expected her to be tanned and glowing from her holiday, but her fair skin only has a slight tinge of bronze to it, nothing obvious. Her red hair is loosely curled and pinned on one side. She looks effortlessly elegant as always.

"Hi Mia, nice to see you," Jacob says with a forced smile to match mine as he enters the kitchen.

"Yep, you too," I agree awkwardly.

"I do hope Jakey has been taking care of you whilst I have been away, Mia," Elle says without looking up from the stove.

"Well, I have been really busy so haven't seen anyone much," I lie and throw Jacob a worried look.

God, I just want the ground to swallow me up. I've only been here five minutes, and this is already hell on earth. Jacob seems calmer than me, but I can tell from his expression that he is hating every minute.

"Here you go handsome, your favourite," Elle says as she places a bowl down in front of Jacob and kisses his cheek at the same time.

I'm taken aback because I have never seen Elle offer any type of affection and I hate the fact she's just done it now.

Jacob shoots me a regretful look as if he is apologising already. He anxiously bites his bottom lip. He almost looks like he is about to blurt out the truth, but I hope he doesn't.

"So how was Cape Verde?" I ask lightly.

"Oh, it was beautiful! I treated myself to a few goodies and spa treatments, it was just what I needed!"

Elle beams as we all begin eating our soups and she gets to continue to boast about all the amazing facials and treatments she and her friends had together.

I keep smiling and nodding as she chats away, but it's not easy to play along, especially when Jacob's eyes are constantly on me.

Elle doesn't seem to have noticed that, but it makes me worried all the same.

"Oh, and before I forget, Mia, I've done you a huge favour!" Elle suddenly changes the subject and watches me excitedly.

"Oh?" I ask and take a sip of the cheap wine Elle thought I'd love.

"Yes! I got rid of that mangy stray that has been hanging around yours."

I almost choke on the horrifically dry wine.

"Puss?"

"Oh, you named it?" She chuckles in a patronising manner.

Jacob's eyes turn back into those puppy dog eyes, and she recognises my hurt.

"Elle, Puss was my cat. I took her in. She was my friend. My company. I told you this?" I declare, my voice a little shaky.

"Did you? I don't recall." Elle shrugs carelessly.

"It's fine Mia, I'm sure we can call the rescue shelter and explain there's been a mix-up," Jacob suggests.

"You'll have a job! The shelter is miles away and I was far too busy to take her there."

"Where did you take her?" I ask, growing agitated.

"I just drove far enough that she won't bother you anymore and I let her go," she declares, so coldly.

I slump back into my chair as if I have just been winded. Technically, I have. Elle's harsh words have shocked me to the core. How could she do such a heartless thing? Puss was just a defenceless animal, looking for some food and company.

"What the fuck, Elle? Why would you do that?" Jacob says as he drops his spoon into his bowl with a loud clacket.

"I guess hell hath no fury like a woman scorned. Isn't that how the saying goes? Mia, would you say a woman is scorned if she sees the neighbour fucking her husband on the security camera?" Elle casually says with her wine in one hand and her chin resting on her other palm.

She stares at us back and forth, waiting for an answer, as an unnerving smirk spreads across her face.

Oh fuck, this is it. Elle knows.

Chapter forty-one – Jacob's point of view

This is it; I knew a future with Mia wasn't going to come easily but Elle is going to expose me and ruin it.

Once Mia knows what else I am involved in, it'll be over. She'll get up, walk out of here and never turn back.

After all the drama she had with Alex, I won't stand a chance. She won't stick around with me when she knows. I know she won't.

I have never once hated Elle, but right now I am looking at her and all I want to do is shut her up. Her spoiled, immature attitude is in full swing and I hate it.

She's glowing, smiling, even sneering as she sits back, sipping her wine and basking in this moment knowing that she gets to destroy me.

I get it, I deserve it, I know I do, really. I'm a married man and I have been unfaithful. She has every right to be angry, smash my car up, rip my clothes, do whatever else she needs to do to feel better.

But we both know our relationship isn't like that, which is why this isn't fair.
Elle knows that I haven't been happy for a long time and she didn't care. It didn't benefit her to care. As long as I didn't leave her, she had access to money, op-

portunities and the life she wanted.

She got out of me everything she wanted, and I have always accommodated her. I'm offering even now to give her everything.

I'm not looking to hurt her; I know what with the house and the money she'll be happy.

But she's looking to hurt me and for the first time in our relationship, Elle holds all the cards.

"Please..." I plea and look at her straight in the eyes.

She pauses. Staring back, sipping her drink but holding my stare.

"It's just business, Jakey. We all must fully understand the terms and conditions mustn't we." She says with a hurtful smirk and my heart drops knowing that she doesn't care a tiny bit about me, she never did.

The best I can wish for now, is the hope that Mia might at least me give the chance to explain. Maybe if I could tell her how and why it all came about, she might not think I'm the monster Elle is about to paint me out as.

Please, Mia, I think to myself.
Just don't leave me.

Chapter forty-two

"Imagine my surprise when I'm sat poolside with a Mojito in one hand and a good book in the other and then suddenly a warning notification is sent to my phone to let me know there is an intruder in the man cave," Elle begins to explain. She looks at Jacob with an almost proud smile on her face and his expression suddenly changes, as if he has just had some kind of realisation.

"So, the man cave has a special security code on it because of the safe we keep in there. If the code isn't entered upon entry, then a warning is sent to our phones which gives us the option to ask for police assistance. It's really quite a clever idea. Probably one of the best you've had Jacob."

"Okay, Elle, I get it." Jacob sighs impatiently.

"But Mia doesn't. So, shut up and stop interrupting me so rudely. Anyway, so Mia, you can imagine my instant concern. Thankfully, I was relieved to realise it was just a simple issue of my husband being so distracted that he forgot to type in the code. Do you know what distracted him, Mia?"

"Elle, I…"

"It was you," she glares. "My husband forgot to put the code in because he was too busy carrying you onto his sofa. Where he fucked you and you spent the night. Remember?"

I gulp anxiously but nod my head. She watched us. She knows everything, there's no point denying it now.

"And to think, I tried to befriend you and welcome you to the suburbs, but you turned out to be nothing but a filthy two-faced tramp."

"Don't you dare call her that!" Jacob explodes so angrily that Elle falls back in her chair, flummoxed. She studies Jacob carefully and then glances at me before staring in bewilderment back at him.

"Oh my god," she finally says. "This is more than sex, isn't it?"

Her arrogant demeanour and unkind smirk quickly fade.

"We can't keep kidding ourselves Elle. We aren't in love," Jacob says, softening his voice.

She snorts in disbelief.

"And you love her?" She points at me in disgust, to which Jacob nods.

She chugs back the rest of the wine in her glass and pauses whilst her face looks busy with thoughts.

"Okay...we can still salvage this Jacob. I'm willing to overlook the silly crush, or whatever this is, as long as you promise not to do it again," she says oddly smoothly as if we are figuring out what to eat from a takeaway menu.

Jacob shakes his head before she has even finished her sentence.

"No. I'm sorry Elle but I can't stay married to you like this anymore. We don't love each other."

"Think about our families Jacob! We can't be selfish here and embarrass them with a divorce. What would people say? We promised them we would take over the family business one day!" Elle snaps.

"No Elle, I promised them I would take over my family's business one day. You promised your family you would marry well.

There will be someone else for you Elle, it's just not going to be me. I don't want this."

"I won't let this happen. Our families will stop this Jacob! So, let's just stop this craziness right now," she pleads, with the first glimmer of desperation I have heard from her.

"I'll deal with them. It's my decision," Jacob replies firmly and turns to me with a reassuring smile.

I sit awkwardly but quietly whilst I watch on, desperately wishing I wasn't here. Elle sits trying to process it all and Jacob looks strangely calm. Even relieved that the truth is out.

"Elle, I will make this easy on you. You can have the house, the savings, the cars. It'll help you to start again. I won't take anything from you," Jacob offers as he leaves his seat and comes to sit beside me instead, which causes the colour from Elle's rosy cheeks to drain and her jaw to drop open in disbelief.

Elle's arrogant demeanour makes a return as she folds her arms and stares at me smugly.

"It's funny, Mia. I didn't have you pegged for the criminal type."

"Elle, shut up!" Jacob erupts.

"I don't understand?" I say, timidly.

"Ha! Brilliant. Of course, you don't understand." Elle chuckles.

"You didn't tell her, did you Jacob?"

"Tell me what?"

"Aww, I almost don't want to spoil it for you darling. After all, you've been a real fan of the honest and successful lawyer Jacob is. God, it was so cute how you rambled on about his amazing achievements like a silly little fan girl." Elle giggles in a way that makes me feel uneasy.

"I can tell her myself!" Jacob desperately shouts over her.

"But you didn't, did you? So, I guess two of us are in for a surprise tonight."

"You're a cold vile bitch!" Jacob snaps at a smug Elle, but she ignores him.

"Yes, Jacob is a lawyer," she says as she flicks her hair back from her shoulder. "But he is also part of an...an agreement, I guess would be the term for it. Jacob and some other lawyers, judges and even a few police officers regularly help out a well-known gang from North London."

I see out of the corner of my eye that Jacob's head has dropped down in shame.

"What type of agreement?" I croak.

"The type where money is exchanged in return for protection from the law. Jacob here works with the judges and police I mentioned in order to keep this gang out on the streets and not behind bars. He helps botch evidence, lie, bend the rules, pretty much anything they need."

"Jacob?" I ask but the look in his eyes tells me that I don't need to question him. He has guilt written all over him.

"Don't worry though Mia, it's nothing awful. Just drug deals and money laundering mostly. Oh, and there's been the odd murder, hasn't there Jakey?" Elle reveals, smugger than ever.

I look back and forth at them both. Jacob looks ready to fall apart and Elle looks so proud of the bombshell she has just dropped onto me. She stares eagerly, waiting for me to cry, run out of here and abandon Jacob.

And I must admit, I'm close too. I'm scared of what Elle has told me. I'm scared that I am in way over my head now, but I know

I would be more scared to walk out of here and never be with Jacob again.

Or maybe, just maybe, I like the drama more than I care to admit.

"My dad used to say that sometimes good people do bad things, but that doesn't make them like the bad people who do bad things," I finally say, ending the long silence in the room.

"What the hell does that mean?" a frustrated Elle asks as she folds her arms.

"It means I'm not going anywhere," I announce confidently, much to Elle's dismay.

A sigh of relief falls from Jacob's mouth and I smile at him re-assuringly.

"If it's not too much bother Elle, I'd like another glass of wine," I say, with all the smugness and arrogance that she had projected onto me since the day I met her.

But I can't help myself, I am completely and utterly crazily in love.

Printed in Great Britain
by Amazon

62499525R00147